Animal Crackers

Also by Robert Hendrickson

THE GRAND EMPORIUMS

LEWD FOOD

HUMAN WORDS

THE LITERARY LIFE AND
OTHER CURIOSITIES

Animal Crackers
A Bestial Lexicon

Robert Hendrickson

THE VIKING PRESS NEW YORK
PENGUIN BOOKS

Penguin Books Ltd, Harmondsworth,
Middlesex, England
Penguin Books, 40 West 23rd Street,
New York, New York 10010, U.S.A.
Penguin Books Australia Ltd, Ringwood,
Victoria, Australia
Penguin Books Canada Limited, 2801 John Street,
Markham, Ontario, Canada L3R 1B4
Penguin Books (N.Z.) Ltd, 182–190 Wairau Road,
Auckland 10, New Zealand

First published in 1983 in simultaneous hardcover and
paperback editions by The Viking Press and Penguin Books,
40 West 23rd Street, New York, New York 10010

Published simultaneously in Canada

LIBRARY OF CONGRESS CATALOGING IN PUBLICATION DATA
Hendrickson, Robert, 1933–
Animal crackers.
1. English language—Terms and phrases.
2. English language—Etymology.   3. Zoology—
Nomenclature (Popular)   4. Names derived from
animals.   5. Animal lore.   I. Title.
PE1689.H46   428.1   81-23973
ISBN 0-670-12697-7 (hardcover)   AACR2
ISBN 0 14 00.6487 7 (paperback)

Printed in the United States of America by
R. R. Donnelley & Sons Company, Harrisonburg, Virginia
Set in CRT Bodoni Book

Grateful acknowledgment is made to Palmer Price Clark for permission
to reprint a letter; to Gale Research Company for permission to reprint a
selection from *Adventures in Error* by Vilhjalmur Stefansson; and to *Verbatim* for permission to reprint a selection from an article by William
Bancroft Miller, *Verbatim*, February 1977, Copyright © 1977, *Verbatim*. Used by permission.

For
Dorothy Elderd

and in memory of
Laurence Elderd

INTRODUCTION

Ironically enough, this is a book about the great contributions that animals without the power of human speech have
made to the English language, a book that attempts to give
an entertaining, representative sampling of the thousands
of words and phrases owing their origins to these "dumb
creatures." From ancient times such expressions have
been with us. Consider just the avian associations of that
imaginary *nightowl* out on a *lark,* or a *hoot,* celebrating a
promotion, putting a *feather in his cap;* he has just had a
brace of cocktails and is *proud as a peacock,* and, though
somewhat *pigeon-toed, struts* down the street keeping an
eagle eye out for muggers, *watching like a hawk,* until he
decides, rather *crestfallen,* that even if he isn't *chicken-
hearted,* it's impossible to feel *free as a bird* in this part of
town, so he'd better *take flight* in a cab to the family *nest*

before the *hawks* around here are upon him in *one fell swoop,* to *cook his goose* after a *battle royal,* so that he'll be *eating crow* tomorrow instead of being *the cock of the walk.* Doubtless a gross exaggeration, this *old coot*'s tale, but we do use scores of similar phrases every day, often without being aware of it, so subtly ingrained are such expressions in the language.

Animal Crackers is also about the often wonderful ways animals have been named, certainly not by specialists, who, as Kierkegaard wrote, "usually can think of nothing better than calling an animal after their own names," but by ordinary people through the ages. Yet most of all I hope the book will appeal to lovers of animals and words because it is as much fun as both the Marx Brothers' movie and the delicious crackers of our youth that suggested its title. (Edible animal crackers, by the way, have been around for at least a century; there are many more different animals in this book than in a box of them, for the crackers are "dump packed" today, and my kids tell me there are too many kangaroos, tigers, and zebras, hardly any leopards and bears, and nary a giraffe in their boxes!)

In addition to being arranged alphabetically, *Animal Crackers* contains an Animal Name Index including the names of all the animals mentioned, which will give readers a chance to check on the contributions of their favorites to the language. Obviously, a book such as this couldn't have been written without the hundreds of etymological works that preceded it. Sources too numerous to list here have been used, and these have often been cited fully in the text, but where a book has been frequently quoted I have usually referred to it by the author's last name, in which case the following brief reference key will identify the work in question:

BOMBAUGH: C. C. Bombaugh. *Oddities and Curiosities of Words and Literature.* New York: Dover, 1962.

● BREWER: Cobham E. Brewer. *Dictionary of Phrase and Fable*. New York: Harper & Row, 1964.

(●) FARMER: John S. Farmer and W. E. Henley. *Slang and Its Analogues*. 7 vols. New Hyde Park, N.Y.: University Press, 1966.

MATHEWS: Mitford M. Mathews, ed. *Dictionary of Americanisms*. Chicago: University of Chicago Press, 1951.

● MENCKEN: H. L. Mencken. *The American Language*. 3 vols. New York: Alfred A. Knopf, Inc., 1963.

● *OED: Oxford English Dictionary*. 10 vols. London: Oxford University Press, 1888–1935.

● PARTRIDGE: Eric Partridge. *A Dictionary of Slang and Unconventional English*. New York: The Macmillan Company, 1950.

● SHIPLEY: Joseph T. Shipley. *Dictionary of Word Origins*. New York: Littlefield, Adams & Co., 1967.

SKEAT: Walter W. Skeat. *An Etymological Dictionary of the English Language* (revised). London: Oxford University Press, 1963.

WEBSTER'S: *Webster's New Twentieth-Century Dictionary*, Unabridged. 2nd ed. New York: World Publishing Company, 1966.

WEEKLEY: Ernest Weekley. *Concise Etymological Dictionary of Modern English*. New York: E. P. Dutton & Co., Inc., 1924.

● WENTWORTH: Harold Wentworth and Stuart Berg Flexner. *Dictionary of American Slang*. New York: Thomas Y. Crowell Company, 1960.

There are so many animal words and phrases that this book could not possibly be exhaustive and still cost less than fifty dollars; I have had to pick and choose to keep the volume to size while representing as many different animals as possible, as well as terms important in language and history. Certainly I have sinned by omission often, but then *Animal Crackers* is a selection of what just one person considers to be the most interesting, typical, and revealing words of their kind. While trying to be as sententious as possible, I have always tried to include all the possible derivations of an expression—tracking down some of these often took weeks and even months. I hope that readers will enjoy the result and that it will inspire others to make such investigations and discoveries on their own.

I would like to thank here the many people who helped me, from those who suggested words and phrases, to my wife, Marilyn, who shared so much of the research involved, and my editor, Barbara Burn, who helped *lick into shape* these pages. But I'm not trying to *pass the buck,* that's no *bull*; the responsibility for all that's here, every last *canard,* is mine. In any case, I'd better *hightail* it out of here, *like a bat out of hell,* before I wind up *in the doghouse* for getting everything *all balled up;* I'm sure everyone's *at the end of his* or *her rope,* or *tether,* with all this *beating around the bush*—and, quite candidly, I do want to *bring home the bacon!*

—Far Rockaway, N.Y.

Animal Crackers

A AND THE OX

Like Chinese characters today, each letter in our alphabet began with a picture or drawing of an animal, person, or object that eventually became a symbol with little resemblance to the original object depicted. No one is sure what these pictographs represented originally, but scholars have made some educated guesses. *A* probably represented the horns of an ox, drawn first as a *V* with a bar across it like the bar in *A*. This may have been suggested by early plowmen guiding oxen by lines attached to a bar strapped across the animal's horns.

AARON'S SERPENT

Aaron's serpent, denoting a force so powerful as to eliminate all other powers, alludes to the miracle in Exodus

(7:11–12) when the Lord commanded that Aaron cast down his rod before Pharaoh: "Then Pharaoh also called the wise men and the sorcerers: now the magicians of Egypt, they also did in like manner with their enchantments. For they cast down every man his rod, and they became serpents, but Aaron's rod swallowed up their rods."

Linguists have found that the word *tannen* given in the Exodus sources really means "reptile," but there is no chance that *Aaron's reptile* will replace *Aaron's serpent* in the language.

ABET

Abet means to incite, or instigate, to encourage someone to act, often wrongfully, and the word derives from an old command for a dog to "sic 'em" or "go get 'em." The word owes its life to the "sport" of bear-baiting, as popular as cricket in fourteenth- and fifteenth-century England. In bear-baiting a recently trapped bear, starved to make it unnaturally vicious, was chained to a stake or put in a pit, and a pack of dogs was set loose upon it in a fight to the death, which the bear always lost, after inflicting great punishment on the dogs. Spectators who urged the dogs on were said to *abet them, abet* here being the contraction of the Old French *abeter*, "to bait, to hound on," which in turn derived from the Norse *beita*, "to cause to bite." Bear-baiting was virtually a Sunday institution in England for eight hundred years, until it was banned in 1835; Queen Elizabeth once attended a "Bayting" at which thirteen bears were killed. In America, too, bear-baiting was not unknown. California *vaqueros* would rope grizzlies and drag them down the mountains to town plazas, where they would be pitted against dogs and even wildcats during religious festivals.

ACTAEON

The Greek hunter Actaeon came upon Artemis bathing, and, either because he saw her naked or because he had boasted that he was a better hunter than she, the goddess of wildlife (she is called Diana in Roman mythology) changed him into a stag and he was torn to pieces by his own hounds. Because he had had horns—at least for a short time—Actaeon's name became a synonym for a man with an unfaithful wife. In fact, *to actaeon,* now obsolete, was once a verb meaning "to cuckold." No one really knows why horns are a symbol of cuckoldry, but one guess is that stags, which are of course horned, have their harems taken from them in the rutting season by stronger stags. At any rate, *making the horn*—thrusting out a fist with the first and last fingers extended—has been a gesture of contempt, implying a person is cuckold, since Roman times. (See also *Cuckoo.*)

ALBATROSS

The *albatross,* subject of more legends than any other sea-bird, takes its name from a corruption of the Portuguese *alcatraz,* which means "large pelican." Called *gooney birds* because of their clumsy behavior, the big alba-trosses—whose wingspan can reach almost twelve feet, greater than that of any other bird—often lumber about the deck on ships, unable to take off after they land because of the cramped space, and actually get as seasick as any landlubber. Sailors have also hooked them out of the air on baited lines. Another name for them is *mollymawks* or *mollyhawks,* from the Dutch *mollemok,* "stupid gull."

3

Despite their apparent stupidity and stubbornness—nothing can force them to abandon their nesting sites, as the Navy learned at Midway—and their poor flying ability when there is no wind current, albatrosses have managed to thrive.

The many legends about the *Cape Hope sheep* include one that says they sleep in flight (probably because they are master gliders on the wind) and another holding that they are good luck omens, that any sailor who kills an albatross will bring disaster to his ship. When the Ancient Mariner shot an albatross with his crossbow in Coleridge's *Rime of the Ancient Mariner,* terrible luck followed. It's said that Coleridge based the poem on a true story Wordsworth told him about privateer George Shelvocke, who shot a black albatross while rounding Cape Horn in 1720 in the *Speedwell.*

ALL BALLED UP

Dashing through the snow on a sled pulled by horses could be hazardous in days past. One difficulty was the balls of snow or ice that formed in the curve of a horse's shoe and often made the horse slip and fall. When horses did fall, especially a team of them, the resulting confusion and entanglement gave rise to the expression *all balled up.* That is, *almost* everybody traces this term for helpless confusion to floundering horses. Mencken suggests a connection with the ejaculation *balls!* (1890), a connection for which little proof can be found. A second alternative, linking the expression to balls of knitting yarn that the cat got at, is a possibility, too. *Balls* has been American slang for testicles since the early 1880s and slang for guts or courage only since about 1935.

4

ALLIGATOR

The biggest lizard that the Romans knew was about the size of the forearm and was thus named *lacertus* ("forearm"), which eventually came into Spanish use as *lagarto*. When the Spaniards encountered a huge New World saurian that resembled a lizard, they called it *el lagarto*, "the lizard," putting the definite article before the noun as they are accustomed to do. Englishmen assumed this to be a single word, *elagarto*, which in time became corrupted in speech to *alligator*. This is probably the way the word was born, but much better is an old story about an early explorer sighting the creature and exclaiming, "There's a lagarto!" Less dangerous than the crocodile, the alligator does have a worse "bark"; it is the only reptile capable of making a loud sound. (See also *Crocodile Tears.*)

ANIMAL BLACK ARTS

The Roman *auspex* was a man appointed to foretell the future by observing the flight of birds, listening to their songs, observing the food they ate, or examining their entrails. The name comes from the Latin *avis*, "bird," and *specere*, "to look at." No important enterprise was begun without the auspex's consulting the birds to see if omens were favorable; favorable omens came to be called *auspicious* ones.

In later Roman times the *augur* replaced the auspex as the observer and interpreter of bird signs, his name deriving from the Latin *avis*, "bird," and *garrire*, "to talk or tell." His interpretation was called an *augurism*, which became the English word *augury,* an omen, while the Latin *inaugurare,* "to install an official after consulting the birds," became our word *inaugurate.*

There are a number of specific words for various kinds of animal divination or black arts, several of them following:

> ornithomancy—by bird flights
> alectryomancy—by cocks picking up grain
> hieromancy—by animal entrails
> ichthyomancy—by fishes
> myomancy—by mice

Incidentally, *black arts* as the name for the arts of divination is a mistake, no matter how apt it seems. As Ernest Weekley points out, *black arts* was translated into English directly from the Old French *nigromancie,* divination by means of the dead. But the Old French word itself had been formed in error from the Greco-Latin *necromantia,* meaning the same, people confusing the sound-alike words *necro,* dead, and *niger,* black, and associating black with the dark, secret ways of conjuring. The Greeks and others after them believed that they could divine or foretell the future or discover hidden knowledge in many ways besides the study of corpses. (See also *Bad Luck Birds.*)

ANIMAL PLACES

Chicago is said to be an Indian word meaning "the place of strong smells," or "Skunktown." It is only one of many place names bearing the name of a "dumb" animal. A fascinating collection could be made of the names of these places and their stories. There is, for example, a Cockroach Island in the Virgin Islands; Canada has a town called Dog Pound; and in the United States we have, or had in the past, such fascinating eponyms as Rat Gulch, Rat Portage, Jackass Gulch, Cowhide, Moosejaw, Bullhorn, and at least twenty-three Buffalos. There are at least three Cat Islands in America, and dogs are represented with Dog Island, Dog Lake, Dog Rocks, Dog Keys, and Red Dog, to name but five places. Also represented are the mule, horse, bear, fox, wolf, moose, elk, beaver, goose, otter, squirrel, marten, and a menagerie of other animals.

Some place names derive from the names of *individual* animals. Anyone starting such a collection might do well to begin with Alexander the Great's favorite dog, Peritas, if the traditional story is true that the Conqueror, mourning his pet, renamed an ancient city Peritas in his honor. The tale isn't unlikely, considering that Alexander did name another city after his horse. Bucephalus was Alexander's favorite Thracian charger, a spirited stallion that only the Conqueror could ride and that would kneel down to let his master mount. Alexander alone rode Bucephalus in his campaign to conquer the world and "the bull-headed or bull-courage one" is said to have died of wounds or heart strain after swimming the flooded Jhelum River and then carrying his master in full armor through a hard day's fighting on a hot June day. Bucephalus was about twenty years old when he died. The emperor named the ancient city of Bucephala in northern India in his horse's honor. He might even have built the city as the fabled charger's mausoleum—its site is identified by a mound outside the modern Jhelum.

ANIMAL VERBS AND ADJECTIVES

I'm sure these lists of useful verbs and adjectives named for well-known animals could be greatly expanded, but they are beginnings anyway. Some of the words are defined as separate entries farther on. The adjectives are limited to words without "-like" in them (as in *ratlike*) that mean "like an animal or some characteristic of an animal" (as in *bovine*, "cowlike or fat as a cow").

Verbs

to ape	to gull
to badger	to hawk
to beef	to hog
to bird-dog	to horse around
to buffalo	to jackass around
to bull	to lionize
to clam up	to monkey with
to cock	to parrot
to crane	to peacock
to dog	to rat
to duck	to rook
to ferret	to snake
to flounder	to snipe
to fox	to squirrel away
to gander	to whale
to goose	to wolf

Adjectives

acarine (mitelike)	elephantine (elephantlike)
anguine (snakelike)	equine (horselike)
anserine (gooselike)	feline (catlike)
apian (beelike)	herpestine (mongooselike)
aquiline (eaglelike)	hircine (goatlike)
asinine (asslike)	lacertine (lizardlike)
avian (birdlike)	lemurine (lemurlike)
bovine (cowlike)	leonine (lionlike)
canine (doglike)	lupine (wolflike)
caprine (goatlike)	lutrine (otterlike)
cervine (deerlike)	murine (mouselike)

8

oscine (songbirdlike)
ovine (sheeplike)
pavonine (peacocklike)
piscine (fishlike)
porcine (piglike)
ranine (froglike)
serpentine (serpentlike)
simian (apelike)

suilline (hoglike)
suine (swinelike)
taurine (bull-like)
ursine (bearlike)
vermian (wormlike)
viperine (viperlike)
vulpine (foxlike)
zebrine (zebralike)

ANIMAL WARS

Perhaps this short entry says as much about the nature of war as any ten-volume history. There are to my knowledge only three wars named after animals. One was the *War of the Stray Dog* in 1925, a conflict no more stupid than most wars, which took place when a Greek soldier ran after his dog, which had strayed across the border in Macedonia. A Bulgarian sentry shot the soldier and Greek troops invaded Bulgaria in retaliation. Before the League of Nations intervened over fifty men were killed.

Almost as foolish was the *Emu War*. This took place in 1935 when west Australian farmers, enraged at ostrichlike emus trampling their wheat fields, demanded government help. The government sent troops with machine guns after the birds, which led the soldiers a wild chase through the backcountry for over a month. Twelve emus were killed, several soldiers injured.

The *Grasshopper Battle* was a brief war between the Delaware and Shawnee Indians in 1872 resulting from a quarrel between two children over the ownership of a pet grasshopper. The Delawares won, and the Shawnees moved out of the Pennsylvania territory where the two tribes had long coexisted.

ARACHNIDA, OR
WHY SPIDERS WEAVE WEBS

Arachnida, the class of spiders (plus scorpions and mites), takes its name from the Lydian maiden Arachne, so skilled at weaving that she challenged Athena, goddess of the household arts, to a contest. Athena won the contest, weaving perfect tapestries that told glorious stories about the gods, while Arachne's excellent but imperfect efforts were unflattering to the gods. The proud Arachne, frightened when Athena tore her impious work to pieces, tried to hang herself, but the goddess interceded, changing her into a spider (Greek *arachne*) so that she would forever weave her beautiful designs. Yet she really wants no more of her weaving, legend says, and keeps trying to hang herself—the reason spiders hang on threads from their webs.

ARCTIC

Arctic for "far north" derives from *arctos,* the Greek word for bear. The Greeks referred to the north as *arctos* because the Great Bear constellation (*Ursa Major*) is the most prominent one in northern skies.

AS POOR AS JOB'S TURKEY

Job didn't have any turkeys as far as we know—at least they aren't mentioned in the Book of Job. He certainly was poor and miserable, though, which inspired nineteenth-century Canadian humorist Thomas Haliburton to coin this expression, meaning someone even poorer than Job. Haliburton influenced such vastly different authors as Longfellow and Mark Twain. In one of his Sam Slick tales he wrote about *Job's turkey,* which had but one feather and was so starved that it had to support itself against the barn when it wanted to gobble. Incidentally, the turkey and the dog are the only two animals ever domesticated north of Mexico by American Indians.

AT LOGGERHEADS

Loggerheads are marine turtles found in warm parts of the Atlantic, but the big, knobby-headed snapping turtles have nothing to do with the origin of the expression *at loggerheads,* "engaged in a violent quarrel, or a dispute." At loggerheads seems to refer to medieval naval battles during which sailors bashed each other with murderous instruments called loggerheads. A loggerhead was a long-handled device with a solid ball of iron on the end that was heated and used to melt pitch or tar, which would be flung at the enemy. The loggerheads themselves apparently made for handy lethal weapons *after* the boiling pitch was used up, and mariners from opposing ships probably engaged each other with them, being at loggerheads. Loggerhead also has an earlier meaning of "an ignorant blockhead, a knucklehead," and this idea of stupidity most likely contributed to the popularity of a phrase that suggests that the people at loggerheads in a dispute are headstrong and unwilling to compromise. The marine loggerhead turtles may have been so named because the snapping turtles are a combative breed when handled.

AT ONE FELL SWOOP

The first use of the phrase *at one fell swoop* in English appears to be by Shakespeare in *Macbeth,* where he describes a hellkite killing chickens. But the word *swoop,* referring to a bird of prey falling suddenly on its victims, occurs in an earlier reference to a fabled bird of Madagascar that could swoop down and carry off "a horse and his rider, or an elephant." One fell swoop means a sudden single strike or blow, fierce and often brutal. The *fell* in the phrase has nothing to do with the verb *fall,* as might be suspected, deriving instead from the old English adjective *fell,* meaning "fierce, savage, ruthless," which formed the basis for the word *felon. Swoop* comes from a Scandinavian word that means to move in a stately manner, to sweep along as with trailing garments.

AT THE END OF HIS ROPE

An executed murderer dangling at the end of a rope didn't inspire this old saying for someone who has outrun fortune or exhausted all his resources. It derives from the earlier phrase *at the end of his tether,* which refers to an animal who has come to the end of the rope he is tied to and can graze no more. The exact words aren't recorded in English until 1809, but similar expressions were common as early as the sixteenth century, and Locke used something like it in his *Essay Concerning Human Understanding.* The expression *give him enough rope and he'll hang himself* probably reinforced the stronger meaning of the phrase.

BAD LUCK BIRDS

Birds that appeared to the right of the augur who stood on Rome's Capitoline Hill were considered good luck, and any bird that appeared on his left was said to indicate bad luck. It is from the ceremony of this Roman religious official and fortune-teller that we get the phrase *bird of ill omen*, which is still applied to a bearer of bad news or an unlucky person. Specific birds that have been considered unlucky over the years include the owl, which is said to screech when bad weather (and hence sickness) is coming, the raven and the vulture, held to indicate death, as well as the crow and the albatross (*q.v.*) under certain circumstances. (See also *Animal Black Arts.*)

13

TO BADGER

Badger-baiting consisted of putting a badger in a barrel or hole and setting dogs on him to "worry him out"; the cruel process was repeated several times until the animal died. This ancient "sport" gave us the verb *to badger,* to worry or tease, even though the dogs, not the badger, did the badgering. Centuries later *badger* was applied to the badger game performed by American confidence men and women. Commonly, the woman member of the team in this con game pretends to fall for her victim and goes to bed with him. While they are having intercourse, the male member of the team surprises them, playing the part of the outraged husband. The victim is badgered by the "husband," who finally agrees to accept money as compensation for the wrong done him. It is sometimes months before the victim realizes he is being falsely blackmailed, and even then he often keeps on making payments to avoid publicity. Figuratively, the expression *badger game* is used to indicate any deception for personal or political gain.

Badger is also the nickname of a resident of Wisconsin, either because the state has an abundance of badgers or because the pioneer workers in zinc mines were "dug in" like badgers for the winter, often living underground. Use of the word *badger* for a dealer in grain is of uncertain origin. One folk etymology says that the little animal, which probably takes its name from the white "badge" on its head, got its name from grain dealers because it ate so much grain—as much as the grain dealers stole. The tale is without basis in fact, however. The grain dealer *badger* may take his name, through rhyming slang, from the *cadger,* another middleman in the grain business during the sixteenth century.

BARKING UP THE WRONG TREE

Coon dogs, which can be almost any breed of dog or even a mongrel, commonly chase raccoons through the underbrush and tree them, barking furiously at the base of the tree until their masters come to shoot the gone coon. But the crafty nocturnal animal, called a *rahaugum* by John Smith, often escapes through the branches to another tree in the dark, leaving the dogs *barking up the wrong tree*, which is the origin of the American phrase. Skilled hunters who can *bark* a squirrel, that is, strike the bark on the lower side of the branch where it sits, killing it by the concussion, have nothing at all to do with the expression.

The *bark* of a tree comes to us from the Anglo-Saxon *beorc*, while a dog's *bark* is related to the Old English *barki*, windpipe. It's said that dogs in the wild state howl, whine, and growl, but that their barking is an acquired habit. *Barkable* is an unusual old word. One would take the adjective to be a modern affectation, but it dates back to at least the thirteenth century—a treatise of the time on estate management advised lords to have "discreet shepherds . . . with good *barkable* dogs."

BARNACLE

Fables were frequently invented in ancient times to explain the unknown. This was the case with the ubiquitous barnacle (the average square mile of beach contains at least two billion of its kind), whose very name derives from such a legend.

The *barnacle* was named after the barnacle goose,

which is so called because of its bare neck, *birnake* in Middle English. The breeding habits of these birds were unknown in olden days, and people firmly believed that they were born from what we now know as barnacles. "They are found in north parts of Scotland," proclaimed one of the first "scientific" descriptions of barnacles, "certain shell fishes of a white colour . . . wherein are contained little living creatures; which shells in time of maturitie do open, and out of them grow these little living fowls whom we call barnacle geese."

A glance at a ship barnacle, which causes damage to ships and piers exceeding one billion dollars annually, does show how easily sound observation can lead to the wrong conclusions. The barnacle's long stalk and rounded body clearly resemble the neck and body of a goose, and its tentacles waving during the feeding process suggest the wings of an infant bird being born from a shell and straining out to sea. The belief was so widely held in its day that Shakespeare made reference to it in one of his plays.

The crustacean takes its scientific name, Cirripedia, from the Greek *cirri,* feetlike curls of hair, in reference to its tentacles. Mocha Dick, the real-life whale whose exploits inspired Melville's *Moby-Dick,* probably appeared white because of the many barnacles covering his ancient hide.

BASILISK

Basilisk is another name for the legendary cockatrice (*q.v.*). The two names seem to have been interchangeable and the same myths applied to both beasts. Just to look into the basilisk's eyes was enough to kill a person, and this serpent hatched from a cock's egg had breath so fiery that it killed off all vegetation. The basilisk took its name from the Greek *basiliskos,* little king, in reference to the cock's crest on its head that resembled a crown— the mythical creature had a cock's head, a dragon's tail, and bird's wings. The monster's killing glance led to the use of *basilisk* for the killing glance of a wanton woman, whom you never looked at while making love, and the term *cockatrice* for a prostitute or whore. Today basilisk is the name of a real South American lizard, a harmless, two-foot-long creature that has a crest on its head.

LIKE A BAT OUT OF HELL

Since bats are nocturnal creatures that loathe the light, the hellfires of the infernal regions would inspire them to flap like hell to get out of there. That may be the idea behind the expression to move *like a bat out of hell,* extremely fast, which has been traced to 1908 and which probably goes back to the late nineteenth century. It was also slang used by RAF pilots since World War I for "to fly extremely fast."

BATS IN YOUR BELFRY

Blind bats flapping about in the vast emptiness of somebody's head, which suggested a church bell tower or belfry to someone, form the basis of this expression meaning a little crazy in the head. Apparently no one said *you've got bats in your belfry* until early in this century, for the first recorded use of the words is 1907, when Ambrose Bierce may have invented them. *Bats,* meaning crazy or nuts, seems to derive from the phrase, as does *batty,* meaning

17

the same. The expression holds on mainly because of its alliteration, like the much older *bee in one's bonnet* (*q.v.*).

BATTERING RAM

The Romans called this device for battering down the walls of an enemy city an *aries* (ram), alluding to the male sheep and its powerful butting horns, and our term *ram* or *battering ram* is just a translation of the Latin term. The long log, sometimes hung on chains, was used until the invention of the cannon and has been depicted in hundreds of film epics. It has never been shown, however, in the form of a huge ram's head, although some ancient armies actually constructed it that way.

BATTING EYELIDS

Batting your eyelids is fluttering them. The expression is an American one that goes back to the late nineteenth century and has nothing to do with bats flapping in a cave, someone "gone batty," or even baseball bats. *Batting* in this case comes from the lexicon of falconry in Tudor times. According to a falconry book written in 1615: "Batting, or to bat, is when a Hawke fluttereth with his wings either from the porch or the man's fist, striving, as it were, to fly away." The old word had long been used by sportsmen, and some American wordmonger found a fresh use for it in the 1880s.

BATTLE ROYAL

Cockfighting has a lot to do with this metaphor for a free-for-all, a battle in which more than two contestants are involved, but it probably didn't originate with the now outlawed "sport," as is often stated. The earliest quotations using the phrase *battle royal* support the theory that it derives from medieval jousting tournaments, where it was used to describe two sides fighting, each commanded by a king. Later, the expression became cockpit jargon before passing into standard English. In cockfighting battle royal better describes what we mean by a battle royal today. It was an elimination tournament for gamecocks in which only the best fighters survived. A number of cocks, say eight, were thrown in the pit. These eight fought until there were only four left. Then the remaining four were rested and pitted against each other until two survived. The two survivors finally fought for the championship.

Ralph Ellison used the title "Battle Royal" for a famous story that has nothing to do with either cockfighting or jousting.

TO BAWL OUT

The present meaning of *to bawl out,* to scold someone in a loud voice and a bullying manner, was clearly foreshadowed by Thackeray in *Pendennis* (1850), when he wrote " 'I will fling you out the window . . .' bawled out Mr. Pendennis." *Bawl* for a loud, rough cry goes back to the fifteenth century and probably derives from the Latin for *baulare,* to bark like a dog. The word first meant to bark or howl the way a dog does, but it was also applied to the

19

sounds of other animals, especially cows and bulls. This supports the theory that *to bawl out* originated as American ranch slang, suggested by the bawling or bellowing of angry bulls. The first recorded use of the expression is by Rex Beach in his novel *The Barrier* (1908): "If you'll go back on your word like this you'll 'bawl me out' before the priest."

TO BE AT LOOSE ENDS

There are at least two good explanations for our expression meaning not knowing what to do with oneself. The saying dates back to the middle of the last century in England and was originally *to be at loose end.* One theory connects it with a string hanging loose from a garment, the end attached to nothing. But Ernest Weekley in his *Etymological Dictionary of Modern English* says the phrase suggests "freedom from tether," like that of a horse put out to pasture, out of harness, untied and unemployed.

TO BEAT AROUND THE BUSH

It's hard not *to beat around the bush* about the origins of this one. Hunters once hired beaters who "started" birds and other game for them by beating the bush and scaring them out into the open. The simplest explanation for the phrase *to beat around the bush,* to approach a matter very carefully or in a roundabout way, is that these beaters had to take great care when approaching the bush or they would "start" the game too soon for the hunter to get a good shot. But Ernest Weekley and others contend that the expression, which dates back to at least the early sixteenth century, is a mixed metaphor. Weekley suggests that the old proverb "I will not beat the bush that another may have the bird" joined with *to go around the bush*—an early expression used for a hound hesitating when circling the bush—and gave us *to beat around the bush.* A hound would probably have a better chance to hesitate in this situation than a clumsier man would.

A BEE IN ONE'S BONNET

Ah! woe is mee,
woe, woe is mee
Alack and well-a-day!
For pity, sir, find out the bee,
Which bore my love away.
I'le seek him in your bonnet brave,
I'le seek him in your eyes.

Robert Herrick's little-known poem "Mad Maid's Song," above, written in 1648, is supposed to be the basis for the expression *to have a bee in one's bonnet,* to be slightly eccentric or, especially, to be obsessed with one idea. If the gentleman in the poem is implying in the last two lines that the mad maid is slightly insane, this is the case. Herrick was probably playing with an older expression, *to have bees in the head* or *brain,* which means the same and dates back to the early sixteenth century. Bees humming in the head obviously suggested an obsessive idea busy at work there. A bonnet, at the time, was either a man's or woman's hat.

BEETLE

Beetles, born to bite, take their name from the Old English word *bitula,* meaning "biter." The species of beetles called *dermestes* derive their name from the Greek words for "skin or leather" and "to eat," meaning that an entomologist-etymologist in the early nineteenth century observed that they ate even the hides of dead animals. *Dermestes* are interesting little beetles that *play possum* (*q.v.*) when touched. Actually, their larvae do the eating, and they demolish everything on a dead animal. They're so thorough that large museums sometimes keep a colony on hand to clean delicate specimens to the bone instead of risking chemical or mechanical means. As one writer punned, they're the best way to skin a cat. (See *More Than One Way to Skin a Cat.*)

A BEGGAR ON HORSEBACK

"Beggars mounted run their horses to death," Shakespeare wrote in *Henry VI*, Part III. "Set a beggar on horseback and he will ride a gallop," Robert Burton observed not much later in his *Anatomy of Melancholy,* and Cervantes said much the same in *Don Quixote.* But the proverb, meaning there is no one so arrogant as a beggar who has suddenly made his fortune, probably dates back before either of these writers. It may derive from the old English proverb "Set a beggar on horseback and he'll ride to the devil." The proverb is in fact common to many languages, its German equivalent, for instance, being "Set a beggar on horseback and he'll outride the devil."

TO BELL THE CAT

To bell the cat is, in nonhumorous usage, to take on a dangerous mission at great personal risk for the benefit of others. Cats, of course, have long been belled to prevent them from killing songbirds. But the expression derives from a wise mouse. It is from an Aesopian fable retold in William "Long Will" Langland's alliterative poem *The Vision concerning Piers Plowman,* which was written, as far as is known, between 1360 and 1399. *Piers Plowman* tells of a family of mice who hold a meeting to decide what to do about a cat who has been preventing them from foraging for food. One cunning mouse suggests that a brass bell be hung around the cat's neck so that they would be warned of his approach. All agree that this plan is perfect, except for one sage mouse, who steps forward and says, "Excellent idea, but who will bell the cat?"

BELLWETHER

Since Anglo-Saxon times a *bellwether* has been a castrated male sheep that usually has a bell fastened around its neck and leads the flock. Later the word was applied humorously to a ringleader, the leader of any mob, conspiracy, or the like; then it was used to describe any leader who assumes the forefront of a profession or industry, as in, "Penguin remains the bellwether of paperback publishing," or, "New York is the bellwether of the publishing industry."

A BIRD IN HAND

This proverbial expression can be traced back in English to the early sixteenth century, when it is rendered as "A byrde yn hande ys better than three yn in the wode," and probably much earlier, counting variations such as, "Some bete the bush and some the byrdes take" (1440). Later, Cervantes used it in *Don Quixote* in the full form best known today: "A bird in the hand is worth two in the bush." Actually, the proverb, which is found in German, French, Italian, and several other languages, has its direct ancestor in an ancient saying from Plutarch's *Of Garrulity,* written in about A.D. 100: "He is a fool who lets slip a bird in the hand for a bird in the bush." It is what Ernest Weekley calls one of those proverbial expressions "which contain the wisdom of the ages."

Bird in Hand is today the name of a town in Lancaster County, Pennsylvania, part of the famous Pennsylvania Dutch cluster that boasts towns with unique names like Baresville, Mount Joy, Intercourse, Paradise, and Blue Ball. Many of these places took their names from old inn signs; Intercourse remains unexplained, but thousands of tourists go out of the way to send postcards from the village.

BLACK SHEEP

In times past black sheep were thought to bear the devil's mark in their wool. The superstition arose in days when dyestuffs were so ineffective and expensive that it wasn't practical to dye the wool of black sheep. Since black sheep were biological rarities, there weren't enough of them to market black wool, and the animals were regarded as

24

practically worthless. Generations of farmers cursing their bad luck for having black sheep in their flocks evolved the term *black sheep* for any disgrace in a family or community. Wild sheep are usually brownish, and American mountain men called the buff wool of the bighorn (*Ovis canadensis*) its "long underwear."

BLIND PIG, BLIND TIGER

No doubt these names for speakeasies serving illegal liquor during Prohibition owe much of their popularity to the fact that people believed the rotgut served therein would blind you or get you blind drunk. The names, however, may have more interesting origins. *Blind pig* is traditionally said to derive from the nickname of a band of soldiers called the Public Guard serving in Richmond, Virginia, in about 1858. Their militia hats had the initials P.G. on them, the sobriquet arising because "P.G. is a pig without an *i*, and a pig without an *eye* is a blind pig." One would have to assume that the soldiers were much disliked and were drunk a lot of the time—the saloons they drank in being named after them—to accept this theory, which has law officers being called "pigs" long before the sixties, as indeed they were. The theory seems all the more unlikely when it is known that *blind pig* is recorded as early as 1840, eighteen years before the Richmond Public Guard was formed.

Blind tiger (1857) possibly takes its name from the saloons in faro gambling establishments a century ago, the game of faro being commonly known as *tiger*. But it is just as good a guess to say that both names were suggested by saloons serving cheap booze that got people *blind* drunk—as sloppy drunk as a pig, or as violently drunk as a tiger.

BOLL WEEVIL

Weevil comes from the Old English *wifel*, "beetle"; and *boll*, first spelled *bowl*, refers to the pod or bull of the cotton plant, which the beetle attacks. In Enterprise, Alabama, there is a monument to a boll weevil—erected at the turn of the century after the boll weevil so devastated the cotton crop in the area that farmers were forced to plant peanuts and as a result became more prosperous than they ever had been as cotton planters. (See also *Gull.*)

(TO HAVE) A BONE TO PICK

Tireless mythmakers suggest that *to have a bone to pick* arose from an old Sicilian custom in which the father of the bride gave the bridegroom a bone to pick clean as a symbol of the difficult task of marriage that he was undertaking. But if such a custom existed it has nothing to do with the phrase, which in modern usage means to have an argument to settle with someone. The expression, though its meaning has varied over the years, is some four centuries old and was probably suggested by two dogs fighting over a single bone tossed between them—*a bone of contention*—or by a dog preoccupied with a bone, which suggested the phrase's original meaning—to mull over something.

BOOBIES

Booby, for a dunce, a nincompoop, is recorded in English as far back as 1599, probably deriving from the Spanish

26

bobo, "a fool," which, in turn, may come from the Latin *balbus,* "stammering." It explains later expressions like *booby prize* (c. 1900), a prize of little value given to the loser of a game, and *booby trap* (c. 1850), a trap set for fools. The last originally described practical jokes played by English schoolboys (balancing a pail of water atop a door that a *booby* would open wider, et cetera), but in World War I booby traps became lethal explosive devices, killing wise men and poets as well as fools.

Booby hatch, for an insane asylum, may have its beginnings in the booby hatch, a police wagon used to carry criminals to jail. This term can be traced back to 1776, and certainly some of the criminals confined (for a short time, anyway) in booby hatches were deranged. Further, a booby hatch was a police cell in the late nineteenth century—before some unknown American wit coined *booby hatch.* The term may have been suggested, however, simply from the idea of boobies confined or crammed under a hatch in some snake pit of an early insane asylum.

Boob became the shortened version of *booby* in about 1900, which gave Mencken the chance to coin *boobery, Boobus Americanus, homo boobiens,* and *booboisie,* to describe the ignorant and uncivilized bourgeoisie or Babbitts he baited and barbed.

Booby is also the name of several species of the gannet family, especially the booby gannet of the South Atlantic coast; the bird proclaims itself a true booby by its lumbering flight and monotonous cry, but it was christened *booby* by sailors long ago who noted how foolishly tame it was. It was the brown booby (*Sula leucogaster*), not the so-called blue-footed booby, that gave the bird its name. The grunting or braying brown boobies will not even fly away from men attacking them but try to drive off intruders with their bills.

27

TO BRING HOME THE BACON

In Olde England any married couple who swore that they hadn't quarreled for over a year, or at any time wished themselves "single again"—and could prove this to the satisfaction of a mock jury sometimes composed of six bachelors and six maidens—was entitled to the famed Dunmow Flitch, a prize consisting of a side of bacon that was awarded at the church of Dunmow in Essex County. The custom was initiated in 1111 and lasted until late in the eighteenth century. Although the expression *to bring home the bacon,* "to win the prize," isn't recorded until 1925, *bacon* was used as a word for "prize" centuries before, and most scholars believe that the Dunmow Flitch is responsible for the usage. This custom and the popular American one of awarding the pig he caught to the winner of greased-pig events at county fairs give us the phrase.

BRUIN, CHANTICLEER

Our words *bruin* for a bear and *chanticleer* for a cock come from the Renard (or Renart) the Fox tales that were first told in France in the tenth century and were spread orally all over Europe. Renard, who became Reynard in English, was the narrator of these stories, and they are chiefly concerned with his adventures, especially the sly tricks he plays on the other animals.

The Swiss capital, Bern, takes its name from the Swiss word for bear.

BRUMBY

In Australia a wild horse is often called a *brumby* or *brumbie*. The word possibly derives from the name of Major William Brumby, an early-nineteenth-century settler from England whose descendants still live in Australia. Major Brumby was a noted breeder of horses, but much of his stock escaped and ran wild. *Brumby* may come, however, from the Aborigine *booramby,* meaning "wild."

BUCK, TO PASS THE BUCK

For less than a *buck* here are two good theories about the origins of this slang word for a dollar, which has been around for well over a century:

Animal skins were classified as "bucks" and "does." The bucks, larger and more valuable, became a part of early American business terminology (c. 1800) and later became slang for a dollar.

Or: A marker called a "buck" was placed next to a poker player in the heyday of the game to remind him that it was his turn to deal next. When silver dollars were used as the markers, they took the name *buck* for their own.

Paper markers called bucks may or may not have given us the word for a dollar, but they are almost certainly responsible for the expression *to pass the buck,* to evade responsibility—poker players passed on the responsibility for the deal when they passed the buck.

The mystery about the origin of *buck* might be solved if we knew what was used for the buck or marker in poker. Was it originally buckshot, or was it a buckhorn pointed knife called a "buck" that gave its name to the silver dol-

lars later used for markers? Or was it simply the silver dollar—already called a *buck* after the "buck" skins fron-
tiersmen traded? No answer seems imminent.

BUFFALO

Most people believe that *buffalo* is a misnomer, a name applied with zoological inexactitude to the American bison.
Cortés described the creature as "a rare Mexican bull, with
crooked shoulders, a hump on its back like a camel and
with hair like a lion," but later explorers thought it was the
Asian or African water buffalo and called it after the Spanish *búfalo*, already used in Europe as the name for those
animals. Actually the water buffalo and the American buffalo both belong to the bison family, so if one can bear the
name buffalo the other can too. The mistake early explorers made was in claiming that the native American animal
was the water buffalo and not qualifying it with a name like
prairie buffalo.

Before we all but wiped them out there were more buffalo on earth than humans, great herds of them numbering
over 60 million, spreading out ten miles in every direction.
The immense herds, ranging from Buffalo, New York,
west, were virtually eliminated as a major food source in a
planned government policy to exterminate the American
Indian for the benefit of the advanced civilization everyone
is trying to escape today. All that remains of them are
herds protected by the U.S. Government, but fortunately
these are thriving (up to 10,000 from less than 800 at the
turn of the century), and scientists are trying to cross bison
with beef cattle (the hybrid called a *beefalo*) for future
generations.

Surprisingly, buffalo were hard to kill individually; they
ran at close to fifty miles an hour, were ornery and yearned

for a night, and hunters often pumped half a dozen rounds into their heads without hitting a vital spot. For this reason *to buffalo* became a term for to baffle or confuse and to intimidate by a display of power. But the hunters found ways to slaughter the vast herds, our "Buffalo Bills" often taking only their hides and delicate tongues and leaving the rest to rot. ("Buffalo Bill" Cody won his title by killing sixty-nine buffalo within eight hours in a railroad contest.) So many hides were taken that *buffcoats* made of them became very fashionable, the undyed yellowish coats giving us the word *buff,* and the verb *to buff,* "to polish," entering the language from the strips of buffalo hide that were used to bring metals like bronze to a high polish. Even the word *buff* for an avid devotee of some activity or subject owes its life to buffalo. Buffalo robes were the winter gear of firemen in the middle of the last century. The amateur firefighters who rushed to blazes emulated the professionals by wearing buffcoats made of buffalo skins and were called *buffs* as a result. As for *in the buff,* in the nude or bare skin, this derives from the soft yellow *buff* skins made from buffalo hides that look something like bare human skin tanned by the sun.

In addition, the magnificent buffalo is responsible for all the *Bull-* names (Sitting Bull, White Bull, and so on) of the Great Plains Indian chiefs and warriors. Black American soldiers were called *buffalo soldiers* by the Indians in the West because the short curly hair of some resembled buffalo hair. Sad to say, the Indians weren't always great conservationists of the buffalo, either. The Sioux, for example, often drove entire herds over cliffs and slaughtered great numbers of the beasts just for their tongues.

BUG WORDS

The word *bug* originally had nothing to do with insects, probably deriving from the Welsh *bwg,* "a specter or a ghost." How bug came to mean insect (insect is short for the Latin *animal insectum,* an animal notched or cut into near the middle) no one knows, but perhaps the beetles and other insects first called bugs terrified some people, suggesting supernatural creatures.

Bug in the sense of a ghost or goblin hasn't been used for centuries, except in words like *bugbear, bugaboo,* and *bogey.* A bugbear, an object of terror, usually imaginary terror, was originally a hobgoblin in the shape of a bear that ate up bad children. Bugaboo means the same, probably an American variation on bugbear employing the *Boo!* long used to scare children. Bogey, another word for an imaginary or real thing that causes fear or worry, may be just a dialectical form of the old word *bug,* "ghost or specter," and it gives us both the *bogeyman* used to scare children and the golf term *bogey,* one stroke over par, which arose from a popular 1890 song called "Colonel Bogey." This latter term at first meant "par" in England, because Colonel Bogey's name was adopted by golfers to signify a fictitious gentleman who could play a course or hole in the lowest number of strokes that a good golfer could play it in. American golfers, satisfied with *par* to express the British meaning of bogey, made Colonel Bogey something of a duffer.

The horse carriage *buggy* is also thought to derive from the old meaning of *bug*—the light carriages were called *bogies* (which later became *buggies*) because they were so fast that they scared people out of their wits.

A *bug-eyed* person, someone with protruding eyeballs,

simply has eyes that resemble those of certain bugs, and *bug juice* for cheap liquor is an old term that takes its name from the tobacco-colored secretion of grasshoppers.

Bug in the sense of a defect ("This new model has a lot of *bugs* in it") is most likely a form of bogey, above, in this case a real thing that causes worry, while *to bug* someone, to annoy or worry him, derives either from bogey, or from buggery, sodomy.

The *bug* used to wiretap a telephone or room may also have its origin in bogey, being a device that causes worry, even terror. But the term has its origins in the underworld and could be a shortened form of "burglar alarm"—back in the twenties criminals used to say that premises protected with burglar alarms were *bugged.*

A *bug* in racing terminology means the weight decrease granted to a horse because the jockey riding him is an apprentice; the apprentice jockey himself is also called a *bug.* This term comes from the asterisk appearing on racing forms next to the weight of a horse granted such an allowance. In printing jargon an asterisk, being small, was called a *bug* and the term was adopted by horseplayers.

A *bugologist* is a humorous name for an entomologist, coined back in the last century, as was *bugology,* biology.

To bug out, to retreat hastily, is an expression that dates back to the time of the Korean War, when it was first used by teenagers in America and then in the United Nations "police action" to indicate a military retreat. Since retreats are generally the result of fear, the expression is another one that probably derives in a roundabout way from bugaboo or bogey. Incidentally, the migrating habits of the swan inspired the word *swanning,* "going purposefully anywhere without a purpose," that meant the same thing as *bugging out* during the Korean War.

Firebug best explains those bugs who have enthusiasms often amounting to manias. That this is an old American

33

expression is evidenced by the fact that Oliver Wendell Holmes used it figuratively, writing of "political firebugs" in his *The Poet at the Breakfast-Table* (1872). That is the first recorded use of the term, which generally means a pyromaniac, someone mentally unbalanced who lights fires for his pleasure. But people with a mania for anything have been called *bugs* in America since at least the early nineteenth century; we have had our "slavery bugs," those who wished to see slavery extended into the West, and we still have our "money bugs," whose sole interest is money. Perhaps aberrant passions were originally compared to the voracious appetites of grasshoppers and other bugs that plagued American farmers in the West, insects that are driven to devour everything in sight and give no thought to the consequences. Certainly they were bogeys or bugaboos, "holy terrors" that caused fear and worry to those who observed them or saw the results of their work. From them we probably get the slang words *bugs* and *buggy* for crazy, *bughouse,* "an insane asylum," *bug doctor,* "a psychiatrist," *bug test,* "an I.Q. test," and *bug,* "a crazy idea or obsession." This last use of *bug* yields the expression *a bug up his ass,* "someone with an obsession," and *to put a bug in someone's ear,* "to plant an idea in someone's mind."

One doesn't have to be crazy to be a *bug,* one merely has to do something habitually, as *shutterbug* (camera bug or nut) and scores of similar words attest. *Jitterbug* combines *bug* with the slang word *jitter,* "dancing to swing music." *Litterbug,* meaning someone who habitually litters, is an unknown coinage dating back to the end of World War II, but it owes its popularity to the Lakes and Hills Garden Club of Mount Dora, Florida, which used the slogan "Don't be a litterbug!" in a 1950 roadside cleanup campaign.

The older phrase *as cute as a bug's ear* has nothing to

do with obsessions, it is just the acme of cuteness—if small ears are cute and bugs have ears, what could be cuter than a bug's ear?

TO BUILD (OR SET)
A FIRE UNDER

Mules have been described as the most ornery critters on the top side of the earth, and of course their stubbornness is immortalized in the expression *stubborn as a mule* known to generations. According to one story, they are also responsible for the expression *to build a fire under,* to stir someone to action or movement. Southern farmers, it is said, sometimes built fires under their charges to get the beasts to move when they were standing with all four legs spread and refused to budge despite every other tactic. This was confirmed by Palmer Clark, former research librarian at the Van Noy Library, Fort Belvoir, Virginia, who wrote me that relatives of hers in the "chuggy huggy hills of Tennessee" were familiar with the practice. "Aunt Clellie," Mrs. Clark writes, "said when she was a young girl, loads of cedar were transported to Murfreesboro from Hall's Hill Pike. She distinctly remembered that her brother-in-law . . . literally and actually built fires under the mules who hauled the cedar to get them going (this about 1921 or 1922 in Middle Tennessee)."

Whatever the case, the yarn is worth respinning. A *mule* is probably the offspring of a mare and a male ass, while the offspring of a stallion and a female ass is called a *hinny.* Both are sterile, of course. As Josh Billings wrote in his "Essai on the Meul," a favorite of Lincoln's: "The meul is half hoss, and half jackass, and then kums tu a full stop, natur diskovering her mistake."

35

BULL!

Bull!, in the sense of a lie, an exaggeration, an incredible concocted story, was first recorded in 1911 and is not a euphemism for the euphemistic *booshwah* (which derives from the French *bois de vache,* "cow's wood" or dried dung). It has nothing to do with papal bulls, either, or, for that matter, with Irish bulls (ludicrous incongruities such as "It's grand to be alone, especially if your sweetheart is wid you").

No one can say for sure just how the expression originated. *Bull!* may have passed into English via the French *boule,* meaning fraud. Or it could have come from a *cock and bull story* (*q.v.*) Another explanation is that it is simply a shortening of *bullshit,* which was first recorded in 1928, but was probably around long before that. Still another has it deriving from the American expression "I wouldn't trust him as far as I could throw (fling) a bull," dating back to the 1830s.

Bull session, the term for an informal discussion, isn't heard so much anymore. Today young people generally *rap* rather than *shoot the bull.*

BULL AND BEAR MARKETS

An old fable common to many lands tells of a man who sold his bearskin before he caught his bear. Selling the skin before you catch the bear became proverbial in England and in about 1700 certain speculators in London's Exchange Alley, the Wall Street of its day, were called *bearskin jobbers.* These speculators gambled on a falling market, selling stock they didn't own in the hope that it would drop in value before they had to deliver it to the purchaser, which would net them a handsome profit on the deal. Bearskin jobbers in "the Alley" were especially active during the bursting of the South Sea Bubble of 1720. The bubble burst after shares in the South Seas Company, a company formed to trade with Spanish America, rose from 128 pounds a share in January 1720 to over 1,000 pounds a share by July of that year, the wildest speculation in history, based on the public's exaggerated idea of the wealth trade would bring England once a treaty with Spain was signed. Bearskin jobbers, including directors of the company who had inside knowledge, took advantage of this situation and made quick fortunes when the company failed and stock in it became worthless. The widespread ruin caused by the South Sea scheme made bearskin jobbers a familiar term to Englishmen, and by the twentieth century the name of such speculators was shortened to bears.

Today a *bear* is an investor who sells stock short in the hope of buying it later at a lower price, someone who believes business conditions are becoming unfavorable, and a *bear market* is one in which the majority of investors act and feel this way. A *bull market* is the exact opposite, dominated by *bulls,* investors who purchase stock in anticipation of a rise in its value. These *bulls* weren't given their name until a decade or so after the bearskin jobbers, *bull* in this sense probably referring to the way the aggressive bull pushes forward, always tossing its head upward and tossing things *up* with its horns.

BULL IN A CHINA SHOP

Back in 1936 bandleader Fred Waring lost a bet to actor Paul Douglas and had to lead a bull through Plummer's China Shop in New York City. Waring agreed to make good any damage the bull might do, but Ferdinand walked up and down the aisles with aristocratic grace, whereas his leader knocked over a table of china. Obviously bulls aren't as clumsy and reckless in delicate situations as the old saying holds, but the expression has been common in English since before 1834, when Frederick Marryat used it in his novel *Jacob Faithful*. The *china* in the phrase refers to the fine porcelain from China brought to Europe from the Far East as early as the sixteenth century, and one theory has it that the termination of trade between China and John Bull (England) in 1834 had something to do with the coining of the phrase—perhaps through a political cartoon showing an angry John Bull threatening to destroy a "China" shop if trade wasn't resumed.

BULL'S EYE

There are many plausible ways to explain this term, all of them based on a bull's eye, which is about the same size as the small black spot at the dead center of a target. *Bull's-eye* targets were not used in ancient archery contests, as is commonly thought, but were introduced to England as targets in rifle and handgun competition. Perhaps the bull's eyes in them were simply named for their resemblance to a bull's eye. But it is possible that bull's eyes take their name from a British coin called the *bull's eye,* which was worth a crown, or five shillings. This coin was in circulation in the early 1800s, about the time bull's-eye targets were introduced, and it would seem more logical to name the flat target centers after flat coins than after the round eye of a bull. As for the coin, it was named in the late seventeenth century, possibly because the one-crown piece was often bet on the outcome of a bull-baiting contest between dogs and bull—the coin bet was "put on the bull's eye" when the bull was backed, just as today we put a bet on a horse's nose.

BUSY BEES

That bees are busy there is no doubt—one pound of honey results from the visiting of some ten million flowers where bees collect nectar, which they change to honey in their bodies. People have known this for thousands of years, and no doubt the words *busy as a bee* go back long before we have a record of them in Chaucer's *Canterbury Tales. To make a beeline for,* on the other hand, is an Americanism dating from about 1830. It means the straight route between two points, a quick way, like a bee flying straight for the hive with his honey.

Spelling bee is among the last survivors of a large number of *bees* relating to social gatherings (bees being busy, cooperative, social animals) "for performing some task in common." These are American in origin—the first one recorded is a 1769 *spinning bee* in Taunton, Massachusetts, though the term was in use before that. Later came *bees* prefixed by apple, building, candy, checker, chopping, drawing, housecleaning, husking, knitting, logging, paring, picking, political, quilting, raising, sewing, shingle, shooting, shouting, shucking, spinning, squirrel, stone, tailor, and wood. There were even *rattlesnake bees,* where "the venomous reptiles . . . were summarily excised by fire and lethal weapons"; *kissing bees,* parties for young people; *whipping bees,* where toughs beat someone; and *lynching bees.* The affairs, sometimes called "frolics," were often followed by parties.

39

C AND CAMEL

The letter *C* is probably the highly modified form of an ancient sign for a camel. One of the strangest stories attached to any letter is told about this one. It seems that Admiral George Cockburn led the incendiaries who demolished the *National Intelligencer* when the British burned down Washington during the War of 1812. The gentlemanly incendiary had his men melt down all the *C*s in the newspaper office, "so that later they can't abuse my name."

CAESAR

The great Roman soldier Gaius Julius Caesar, whose name is responsible for more words in our language than any other, may have owed his name to a Punic word meaning "elephant." This was the opinion of Pliny and others, and old Roman coins bearing his name often picture an elephant on one side. Caesar conquered 300 nations, took 800 cities, killed a million men and defeated three million more, and most words deriving from his name reflect his great power. *Caesarea* was an ancient seaport in Israel, the Roman capital of Palestine. The three terms *Caesarism* ("imperialism"), *Caesarist* ("imperialist"), and *Caesarize* ("imperialize") commemorate the first Caesar's adopted son and successor, Augustus, referring to the imperialist government instituted by the first Roman emperor. *Caesaropapism* is the possession of supreme authority over both church and state by one person. Of the many proverbs that recall the great Roman's name the most famous is probably Render therefore unto Caesar the things which are Caesar's; and to God the things which are God's, which is, of course, the familiar biblical injunction (Matthew 22:21) from Jesus to the Pharisees. Then there are cesarean section, Caesar's mushroom (*Amanita caesaria*), the code Caesar cipher, Caesar's wife must be above suspicion, czar, Jersey, kaiser, sherry, and many more. All ultimately from an elephant. (See also *Jersey*.)

CAMELOPARD

The *camelopard* is not any mythical monster, but a very real animal, though you might not have believed it existed if you hadn't seen it in jungle or zoo. The ancient Greeks came across the beast on the African plain and called it *kamelopardalis,* believing it to be a cross between the camel—because of its height—and the leopard—because of its spots. It was called the camelopard in English for many years, beginning in at least 1398, until its present designation began to be used in the late sixteenth century: *giraffe* (from the Arabic word for the animal). The giraffe, the world's tallest animal, at up to twenty feet (so tall that newborn calves come to life with a jolt, falling six feet to the ground), also has the highest blood pressure of any animal (an average 260/160 as opposed to 120/80 in humans) to compensate for the pull of gravity while it is supplying blood to a brain ten feet above the heart. It has the same number of bones in its neck (seven) as a human—longer bones, of course. Though ungainly, the giraffe can be a gently dignified animal. Wrote Isak Dinesen in *Out of Africa:* "I had time after time watched the progression across the plain of the giraffe, in their queer, inimitable, vegetative gracefulness, as if it were not a herd of animals but a family of rare, long-stemmed, speckled gigantic flowers slowly advancing."

CAMEL'S HAIR

A German artist named Kemel may have given his name to *camel's hair* artist's brushes because he invented them, but there is no evidence to support the theory that *camel's hair* is a corruption of *kemel's hair.* In any case, the name camel's hair is a misnomer: the artist's brushes are made from long tail hairs taken from squirrel species inhabiting cold areas like Siberia. Most likely the brushes were erroneously named because people thought they were made from the fine hair of the two-humped Bactrian camels when they were introduced in the eighteenth century. Camel hair, longer than sheep's wool and as fine as silk, had been used in Europe since the early fourteenth century for cloth and other items.

CANARD

The word *canard* refers to something one "canardly" believe, as a punster put it. In French *canard* means "a duck" and the word *canard,* meaning a ridiculously false story, probably comes from the French expression *vendre un canard à moitié,* literally, to half-sell a duck. As a duck flying in the sky can't be half-sold, the expression figuratively means to make a fool out of a buyer or anyone else with a false story. Tellers of "half-ducks" or *canards* were known in France three centuries ago, and the word probably gained a firmer foothold with a hoax played by a Frenchman named Cornelissen. Testing the gullibility of the public, he published a story that he had thirty ducks, one of which he killed and threw to the other twenty-nine, who ate it. Then he cut up a second, then a third, until the twenty-ninth duck was eaten by the survivor—an excellent bull, duck, or canard story.

Another theory is that *canard* is more simply a malapropism derived from the French word *canular* ("hoax").

CANOPY

All *canopies* were originally "gnat curtains," the word deriving from the Greek for "gnat or mosquito." According to Herodotus, Nile fishermen were the first to use canopies, their mesh curtains attached to poles forming a kind of tent under which they could sleep safe from mosquitoes at night. The word was next applied to bed hangings, then to the covering suspended over thrones, and finally to any overhanging protection.

CAPUCHIN

The order of Capuchin monks, established in 1520, came into being when Franciscan friar Matteo di Bascio insisted that the habit worn by the Franciscans wasn't the one that St. Francis had worn. He stubbornly fashioned himself a sharp-pointed pyramidal hood (*capuche*), let his beard grow, and went barefoot; the Pope granted him permission eight years later to wear this costume and form a separate order that would preach to the poor. The new offshoot of Franciscans came to be named for the headdress its monks still wear, and it wasn't long before a woman's combined cloak and hood was dubbed a *capuchin* after the monks' cowl. The word in its latter meaning was used frequently and is even recorded in a bawdy Scottish ballad:

> As Molly Lee came down the street,
> Her capuchin did flee;
> She coost a look behind her
> To see her negligee.

The tropical *Capuchin monkey* and *Capuchin pigeon* are named for the Capuchins' costume—the monkey's black hair and appearance resembling their monastic cowl, and the pigeon having a hoodlike tuft of black feathers.

TO CAST PEARLS
BEFORE SWINE

Sometimes those who say they won't *cast pearls before swine*—that is, they won't offer their poems, art, or whatever to the unappreciative masses—have only paste pearls to cast. If not used humorously the saying is certainly prig-gish and egotistical, as well as offensive to the "swine." It is a familiar biblical injunction, from Matthew 7:6: "Give not that which is holy unto the dogs, neither cast ye your pearls before swine, lest they trample them under their feet, and turn again and rend you." John Wycliffe, commenting on the passage in 1380, added that men should not give holy things to hounds, a phrase that has been used much more sparingly.

A CAT HAS NINE LIVES

Recorded in 1546, this old English saying surely goes back well before the sixteenth century. Cats were regarded as tenacious of life because of their careful, suspicious nature and because they are supple animals that can survive long falls, though not from the top of a skyscraper, as some people believe.

CAT ON A HOT TIN ROOF

Best known today as the title of Tennessee Williams's famous play, the expression has been in wide use in America since the turn of the century. *Like a cat on a hot tin roof* derives from a similar British phrase, *like a cat on hot bricks,* which was first recorded about 1880 and also means someone ill at ease, uncomfortable, not at home in a place or situation.

CATERPILLAR

A *caterpillar* was a *chatepelose,* a "hairy cat," in Old French, and it is from this word that we originally got our word for the "wyrm among fruite," as the English once called the creature. But the meaning and spelling of *caterpillar* were strengthened and changed by two Old English words. *To pill* meant "to strip or plunder," as in *pillage,* which came to be associated with the little worm stripping the bark off trees; and a glutton was a *cater,* which the creature most certainly is. Thus the caterpillar became a "greedy pillager" as well as a "hairy cat," both good descriptions of its mien and manner.

CATGUT

Stray cats aren't killed to get it. *Catgut* is a misnomer; it is actually the intestines of sheep, and sometimes horses and mules, which are used to make the tough cords violins and tennis rackets are strung with (when metal and nylon aren't employed). Probably the word *catgut* was originally *kitgut,* the word *kit* meaning a small fiddle as well as a kitten; but the English word *catlings,* small strings for musical instruments, contributed to the confusion, too. The toughest and best catgut comes from the intestines of lean, poorly fed animals. Roman strings, the best catgut strings for musical instruments, are made in Italy. Catgut is also used for hanging clock weights and for sutures in surgery.

CATHOUSE

Cat was slang for a prostitute as far back as 1401, when a poem of the day warned men to "beware of cats' tails." Although the term associating the cat and commercial sex is obsolete, the connotation hangs on in the word *cathouse* for a bordello, crib, fancy house, whorehouse, or sporting house. A cathouse is usually a cheap bordello. It's anybody's guess whether the cathouses take their names in some obscure way from the old word for harlot or whether they were named independently after the sexual qualities usually attributed to cats. The same applies to *cat wagons*, the mobile brothels of the early West.

CAT-O'-NINE-TAILS

Some black humorist probably coined the name for this terrible scourge—because it "scratched" the back like a cat—but the fact that the first Egyptian scourges were made of thongs of cat hide may have something to do with the word's origin. The nine tails of the scourge being similar to the "nine lives of a cat" could also have suggested the name. Scourging criminal offenders with a whip is a punishment as old as history; there were cases in medieval England of prisoners receiving 60,000 stripes from whips of three lashes with twenty knots in each tail. But the *cat-o'-nine-tails,* composed of one eighteen-inch handle with nine tails and three or more knots on each tail, only dates back to about 1670. Men were flayed alive with this scourge, which people believed was more sacred, and thus more effective, because its nine tails were a "trinity of trinities." The British navy only stopped using the cat-o'-

nine-tails as an instrument of punishment in 1881, and it can still be used in England as a punishment for certain violent crimes, though it rarely is.

CAT'S CRADLE

Word detectives have given *cat's cradle* up as a bad job. The first mention of the child's game is in a little-known book called *The Light of Nature Pursued* (1768), where the author attempts to explain it: "An ingenious play they call cat's cradle; one ties the two ends of a packthread together, and then winds it about his fingers, another with both hands takes it off perhaps in the shape of a gridiron, the first takes it again from him in another form, and so on, alternately changing the packthread into a multitude of figures whose names I forget, it being so many years since I played it myself." According to the experts, the suggestion that the game's name is a corruption of *cratch-cradle,* the manger cradle in which Christ was born, is not founded on facts. The story I was told when a boy had it that the first figure in the game resembled a *cratch,* a medieval English word for a hayrack, while the last figure resembled a cradle. The game was first called cratch-cradle and this was changed to cat's cradle in later years when the hay cratch was no longer used or familiar to people—not because cats had anything to do with the game but because the word *cat* sounded something like *cratch.* I've checked this, and there is an obsolete English word *cratch* for a hayrack, dating back to 1300. Even more pertinent, perhaps, is the fact that *cratch* was before this a verb meaning "to seize, snatch, grab"—so maybe the *cratching* or grabbing of the string became the cat in the name. But perhaps kittens playing with a ball of yarn have something to do with the name of the game. Then again maybe I, too, should give this up as a bad job.

CATTLE, CHATTEL

This is a story of capitalists and cows. *Cattle* is a corruption of the Latin *capitale*, "capital or principal holdings," a word that medieval English peasants found hard to pronounce and altered to *catel* and finally *cattle*. Since the principal holdings of peasants were often livestock, especially cows, *cattle* came to mean what it does today, while the medieval French *chatel*, another corruption of the Latin *capitale*, entered English as *chattel*, our legal term for all personal property.

CAYUSE

Characters in westerns sometimes use the word *cayuse* to describe a horse of little value, but cayuse is strictly a name for Indian ponies, a breed that western pioneers knew as *Kiyuse*, which were rarely properly tamed by white men. The cayuse takes its name from the Cayuse Indians of Oregon and Washington, who bred the small horse. In 1847, blaming whites for a smallpox epidemic, the tribe attacked and killed fourteen missionaries near the present city of Walla Walla, Washington. Subdued and put on a reservation in 1855, their ranks decimated by disease, they died as a people, for no full-blooded Cayuse Indian survives today.

CHAOS CHAOS

Linnaeus discovered and christened this microscopic animal in 1775. It has since been identified only fifty times. The Swedish founder of scientific nomenclature gave the one-celled animal its name because of the chaos it creates. The voracious *Chaos chaos* never fails to attack and destroy all smaller protozoa it encounters.

CHARLEY HORSE

Back in 1946 the *Journal of the American Medical Association* published an article entitled "Treatment of the Charley Horse," rather than "Treatment of Injury to Quadriceps Femoris." This would indicate that *charley horse* has been a part of formal English for almost forty years. But did this term for a muscular leg cramp arise from a lame horse named Charley that pulled a roller across the infield in the Chicago White Sox ball park in the 1890s? That's the old story and there was such a horse, but the expression may have been printed several years before his baseball days, in 1888, to describe a ballplayer's stiffness or lameness. Another derivation that seems likely but hasn't been proved traces charley horse to the constables or *Charleys* of seventeenth-century England. According to this theory, *Charleys* for local police survived in America through the nineteenth century, and, because aching legs were an occupational disease among Charleys, ballplayers suffering such maladies were compared with the coppers and said to be "weary from riding Charley's horse."

CHEAPSKATE

During the Revolutionary War American soldiers liked to sing the Scottish song "Maggie Lauder," the chorus of which chided a *blatherskate,* a gabby person full of nonsense or hot air. The song is a very old one dating back to the seventeenth century and the word *blatherskate* is older still, formed from *bladder,* an obsolete English word for an inflated, pretentious man, a windbag, and a contemptuous use of the word *skate,* referring to the common food fish. Why the *skate* was chosen for the humorous word isn't clear—perhaps because it was believed to inflate itself like a blowfish, or possibly because it was a common fish. In any case, "Maggie Lauder" made *blatherskate* popular here in America, and later in the nineteenth century when we invented our native word *cheapskate* for a tightwad we borrowed the *skate* from it. This is a more roundabout explanation than the theory that the *skate* in cheapskate comes from a British slang word for "chap," but it seems more logical, since *skate* in the form of "chap" never had any real currency here.

CHICKEN FEED

Chickens were fed grain too poor for any other use by American pioneers, and these pieces of poor-quality grain had to be small so the chickens could swallow them. This obviously suggested the contemptuous term *chicken feed* for small change (pennies, nickels, and dimes) to riverboat gamblers fleecing small-town suckers. The first mention of the expression is in *Colonel (Davy) Crockett's Exploits and Adventures in Texas* (1836): "I stood looking on,

seeing him pick up chicken feed from the green horns." By
extension chicken feed has come to mean any small or in-
significant amount of money, and even (rarely today) misleading information deliberately supplied or leaked by a
government to spies employed by another government.

A CHICKEN IN EVERY POT

This synonym for prosperity is often attributed to Herbert
Hoover, and it was indeed a Republican campaign slogan
during the election of 1932, a ridiculous one that helped
the Democrats more than the Republicans with the Great
Depression gripping the land. Some sources credit the
words to Scottish author Alexander Smith, who in 1863
wrote that if the world were ruled by the best men of letters, ignorance would die, war would cease, taxation would
be lightened, and "not only every Frenchman, but every
man in the world would have his hen in the pot." Smith,
however, was clearly referring to Henry IV of France and
his vow on being crowned king in 1589: "If God grants me
the usual length of life, I hope to make France so prosperous that every peasant will have a chicken in his pot on
Sunday." Henry, assassinated in 1610 when only fifty-
seven, wasn't able to provide such prosperity.

CHOW

The *chow* or *chow chow,* a medium-sized, generally red,
black, or brown nonsporting dog of Chinese origin, may
derive its name from *chow,* a pidgin word for food, because
Chinese sometimes ate the dog, or from *chow-chow,* the
Chinese mixed-fruit preserve. Another theory, which

seems more plausible, is that it is simply from the Chinese *Chou,* the ancient Chinese race that formed the Chou Dynasty, which ruled from about 1122 to 256 B.C., bringing about China's first golden age. The chow is noted for its sturdy build, large head, and deep-set eyes. Probably originally bred in northern China, it can be traced as far back as 150 B.C.

CLAM PHRASES

Clams are usually dug at low tide, which explains why *happy as a clam at high tide* means quite happy and content. The expression is an Americanism first noted in 1834. *Close as a clam,* for a mean, stingy person, refers to the difficulty in opening a clamshell and is an older expression that probably originated in England. *Clam up,* an Americanism for to become silent, refuse to disclose information, dates back to 1916 and refers again to the hard-to-open "lips" of the clam. *Clam* for mouth has been common in America since the early nineteenth century.

COCK AND BULL STORY

This long, rambling, unlikely yarn, like the similar canard (*q.v.*) takes its name from the barnyard. The phrase first appeared in about 1600 and has been constantly used ever since; even in classics like Laurence Sterne's *Tristram Shandy* (1767), one of our most imaginative and whimsical novels, where the words end the book: " 'L —— d' said my mother, what is this story all about.' '—A COCK and a BULL,' said Yorick—'and one of the best of its kind,

I ever heard.' " The expression *cock and bull story* hasn't been traced to the specific fable where it originated, but it arose in all probability from a fantastic tale about a cock and bull who talked to each other in human language. Since people knew that such a conversation was impossible, they most likely labeled any incredible yarns cock and bull stories.

Stories of talking animals have been common since the fables of Aesop and in medieval times were collected in volumes called bestiaries, where the behavior of the animals points a moral. Notable ones include Chaucer's Chanticleer story in the "Nun's Priest's Tale," Spenser's "Mother Hubberd's Tale," and Goethe's *Reineke Fuchs*. Modern developments of the form can be found in George Orwell's political satire *Animal Farm* and Richard Adams's *Watership Down*, among many others. The French have used the expression *coq-à-l'âne*—literally "cock to the donkey"—in the same sense as cock and bull for almost four centuries, too. But it is also the term for a satirical verse genre that ridicules the follies and vices of society, deriving in this sense from the old French proverbial expression *c'est bien sauté du coq à l'âne*, which signifies incoherent speech or writing.

COCKATRICE

Thanks to Pliny and other incredulous observers, people were terrified of this fantastic monster with the wings of a bird, the tail of a dragon, and the crested head of a cock until well into the seventeenth century. Said to be born of a cock's egg, the monster was, according to one old description, about "a foot long, with black and yellow skin and fiery red eyes," but others described it as much larger. It could be killed only by the crowing of a cock, and so travelers often carried roosters with them to Africa or wherever they feared a *cockatrice* might be encountered. Otherwise, they believed, just a glance from the fabulous creature's eye could kill them; only the crafty weasel was immune to its "death-rays." But the cock had no part in the naming of the cockatrice. It takes its name from the Greek *ichneumon,* meaning "tracker." This was translated into Latin as *calcatrix,* which was ultimately corrupted to the English *cockatrice.* The mythical creature was called a "tracker" by the Greeks because they believed that it tracked down and devoured the eggs and young of the crocodile. In this respect it was probably given the characteristics of the real Egyptian ichneumon, an animal that does hunt down and devour crocodile eggs. The cockatrice was also confused with a real bird called the trochilus or crocodile bird (*Pluvianus aegypticus*), which often sits on the backs of basking crocodiles and feeds on their insect parasites. The crocodile bird was thought to pick the crocodile's teeth of food, hence its Greek name *trochilus,* the "pick-and-run" bird. This winged dentist might have inspired the myth that both the *ichneumon* and *cockatrice* could dart through a crocodile's open mouth into its stomach and kill it by boring through its belly. (See also *Basilisk; Crocodile Tears.*)

COCKSURE

Since the word *cocksure* first meant secure, safe, and certain—not dogmatic and self-confident as it does today—it probably didn't originally have anything to do with the pompous, strutting rooster usually associated with it. But no one is cocksure about *cocksure*'s origins, which go back almost five centuries. In its now obsolete sense of lecherous, cocksure is much younger, so that eliminates a likely source and a better story. A real possibility is that the word was just a euphemism for *God sure!*—since *cock* was often a euphemism for God in oaths. Or it may have first meant the security of God, as in the following quote from Foxe's *Book of Martyrs* (1563): "Who so dwelleth under . . . the help of the Lord, shall be cock-sure for evermore." Shakespeare uses the word as if it derives from the sureness of the cock on the firelock of a gun, a cock that keeps the gun from going off, and the *OED* suggests as a source the cock or tap on a barrel of whiskey, which secured the liquor inside, preventing its escape. The Welsh word *coc*, "cog," has also been nominated—cocksure would thus mean "as sure as cogs fit into one another." So has the Irish *coc*, "manifest," and the old English *cock* for the notch of a bow—an arrow would have to be set cocksure to hit its target. How many is that, nine or ten possibilities? No matter which is correct, it's almost certain that the idea of the strutting aplomb of a barnyard cock and the phallic associations of the word contributed to its later meaning of pert and cocky.

And if you've ever wondered about names ending in the suffix *-cock*, rest assured that it only means "descendant of." Hancock, for example, means "descendant of little *Hane*," a pet form of John.

A MENAGERIE OF COLLECTIVE NOUNS

Collective nouns are also called terms of venery, group nouns, and nouns of assemblage. Many describing animals are amusing, colorful, and even beautiful, as this list of some 150 terms for over 100 animals amply shows. Most collective nouns make good sense if the animal's habits are known; others can be understood only if their origins are traced in the dictionary (*rag* for colts, for instance, probably derives from an old Norse word meaning "rug" and refers to their coats); and still others continue to stump the best scholars. All of these have been used in ancient or modern times:

Antelope—herd
Ants—colony, swarm, army
Apes—shrewdness
Asses—pace, herd
Bacteria—culture
Badgers—cete
Bass—shoal
Bears—sleuth, sloth
Bees—swarm, grist, hive
Birds—flock, congregation, volary,
    dissimulation
Bitterns—sedge, siege
Boars—sounder, singular
Buffalo—herd
Bucks—brace, clash
Caterpillars—army
Cats—clowder, clutter
Cattle—herd, drove
Chickens—brood, peep
Chicks—clutch
Choughs—chattering
Clams—bed
Colts—rag
Coots—cover
Cows—kine
Cranes—herd, sedge, siege
Crows—murder
Cubs—litter
Curlews—herd
Curs—cowardice

Deer—herd
Dogs—pack
Doves—dule
Ducks—paddling, team (in flight)
Eggs—clutch
Elephants—herd
Elks—gang
Ferrets—business, fesnyng
Finches—charm
Fish—school, shoal, run, haul,
    catch, drought
Flies—swarm
Foxes—skulk, leash
Geese—gaggle, skein (in flight)
Gnats—swarm, cloud, horde
Goats—herd, tribe, trip
Goldfinches—charm
Gorillas—band
Greyhounds—leash
Hares—down, husk
Hawks—cast
Hens—brood
Herons—hedge, siege, sedge
Herrings—shoal
Hogs—drift, passel (parcel)
Horses—harras (enclosure or corral)
Hounds—pack, mute, cry
Jackrabbits—husk
Jellyfish—smack
Kangaroos—troop
Kittens—kindle, litter
Lapwings—deceit
Larks—ascension, exaltation
Leopards—leap, leep
Lions—pride
Locusts—plague

Magpies—tiding
Mallards—sord
Mares—stud
Martens—richness
Moles—labor
Monkeys—troop
Mules—barren, span
Nightingales—watch
Owls—parliament
Oxen—yoke, drove, team, herd
Partridges—covey
Peacocks—muster, ostentation
Peeps—litter
Pheasants—nide, nye, bouquet
Pigeons—flock, flight
Pigs—litter
Pilchards—shoal
Plovers—wing, congregation
Ponies—string
Porpoises—pod, herd
Quail—covey, bevy
Rabbits—nest
Rats—pack, swarm
Ravens—unkindness
Rhinoceroses—crash
Roebucks—bevy
Rooks—building, clamor
Seals—herd, pod
Sheep—flock
Snakes—nest
Snipe—walk, wisp
Sparrows—host
Squirrels—dray
Starlings—murmuration
Storks—mustering
Swallows—flight

Swans——herd, bevy, wedge
Swifts——flock
Swine——sounder, drift
Teal——spring
Toads——knot
Trout——hover
Turkeys——rafter, raft
Turtledoves——pitying, dule
Turtles——bale
Walrus——pod
Whales——school, gam, pod
Wolves——pack, route, herd
Woodcocks——fall
Woodpeckers——descent

TO COME A CROPPER

To come a cropper means "to fall head over heels, to fail or
be struck by some misfortune." This is a British expression
that originally meant only to fall head over heels from a
horse, to fall to the ground completely, neck and crop. But
it most likely refers to the *crop* or rump of a horse——when
a horse falls neck and crop, he falls completely, all together in one heap.

COOK YOUR GOOSE

The Mad King of Sweden, Eric XIV, was so enraged because residents of a medieval town he had attacked hung
out a goose, a symbol of stupidity, to "slyghte his forces"
that he told the residents "[I will] cook your goose" and
proceeded to burn the town to the ground. This story is

generally disregarded because Mad King Eric supposedly avenged his insult in about 1560, and the expression *cook your goose*—to put an end to, to ruin—isn't recorded until 1851. Attempts have been made to relate the phrase to the story of the goose that laid the golden eggs. The peasant couple to whom that goose belonged, you'll remember, killed it (and perhaps cooked it later) because they were eager to get at the golden eggs within its body, which turned out to be undeveloped in any case. But this old Greek fable goes back even further than Mad King Eric. The first use of the phrase *cook your goose* is in a London street ballad condemning "Papal Aggression" when Pope Pius IX tried to strengthen the power of the Catholic Church in England with his appointment of Nicholas Wiseman as English cardinal:

> If they come here we'll cook their goose,
> The Pope and the Cardinal Wiseman.

A COON'S AGE

Meaning "a very long time," *a coon's age* is an Americanism recorded in 1843 and probably related to the old English expression *in a crow's age,* meaning the same. The American term is an improvement, if only because the raccoon usually lives longer—up to thirteen years in the wild—than the crow.

TO COOT

The obsolete verb *to coot,* applied to tortoises, meant to copulate. First recorded in 1667, its origin is unknown, but it is responsible for the name of two amorous American turtles commonly called *cooters*—the Carolina box turtle (*Cistudo carolina*) and the Florida cooter (*Chrysemys concinna*). The first recorded use of the word: "The Tortoises . . . coot for fourteen daies together."

COOTIE

There have been attempts to link this little louse (not flea) with the word *cute* and the English *cootie* meaning "having legs clad with feathers." Partridge seems to be right, however, in tracing the word to the Malayan *kutu* for a dog tick, which "is common throughout Polynesia for any kind of louse." The term was originally used by sailors, was brought here from Polynesia in about 1915, and is mostly used in the plural form—*cooties*—especially by children.

COWLICK

This word for a tuft of hair that stands up and refuses to lie down unless cemented is British in origin. It almost certainly comes from a comparison with the projecting ridge of hairs on a cow's hide, licked into that shape by the animal.

CRAZY AS A LOON

The loon's blood-chilling cry, which progresses from a wailing lament to maniacal laughter, is responsible for its reputation as the epitome of insanity. *Crazy as a loon* is an

Americanism first recorded in 1845. Thoreau encountered a loon at Walden Pond and after telling how the bird could swim underwater—loons can stay submerged up to fifteen minutes and go down eighty feet—he described its laugh:

> His usual note was this demoniac laughter . . . but occasionally, when he balked me most successfully and came up a long way off, he uttered a long-drawn unearthly howl, probably more like a wolf than any bird; as when a beast puts his muzzle to the ground and deliberately howls. This was his looning,—perhaps the wildest sound that is ever heard here, making the woods ring far and wide. I concluded that he laughed in derision of my efforts, confident of his own resources. Though the sky was by this time overcast, the pond was so smooth that I could see where he broke the surface when I did not hear him. . . . At length, having come up fifty rods off, he uttered one of those prolonged howls, as if calling the god of the loons to aid him, and immediately there came a wind from the east and rippled the surface, and filled the whole air with misty rain, and I was impressed as if it were the prayer of the loon answered, and his god was angry with me; and so I left him disappearing far away on the tumultuous surface.

The common loon (*Gavia immer*) is noted for what one expert calls its "mirthless laughter," a "high, far carrying, liquid tremolo that sets your spine atingle." Where the loon's name comes from is not known, although one suggestion is that it derives from the Dutch *loen*, "homo stupidus," and was first applied to stupid people, *then* to the bird. Although the bird is responsible for the phrase *crazy as a loon*, it has nothing to do with *loony*, "crazy," which is a shortening of *lunatic*.

CROCODILE TEARS

Crocodiles can't shed real tears, as they have no tear glands, though their eyes are kept moist by various secretions, and they can appear to be crying when chewing or swallowing, so difficult are these functions for them. Nevertheless, the myth arose in early times that the crocodile moaned and cried to attract the sympathetic and helpful and then snatched and ate its saviors "wepynge" (weeping), as British adventurer and nature faker Sir John Maundeville, the first to record the legend, put it in about 1400. The story was repeated in Hakluyt's *Voyages* (1600) and by many other writers, including Shakespeare, these hypocritical *crocodile's tears* becoming a prop for any feigned or hypocritical sorrow. The crocodile takes its name from the Greek *kroke*, "gravel," and *drilos*, "worm," because the newly hatched animal resembled an oversized worm emerging from gravel on the banks of the Nile to early observers. Many myths exist about the giant lizard, which probably ranks second only to poisonous snakes as a killer of humans. (See also *Alligator, Cockatrice.*)

CRY WOLF

Someone who raises false alarms *cries wolf* like the shepherd boy in Aesop's fable who shouted "Wolf! Wolf!" to make fun of the villagers or attract attention. The villagers, of course, later wouldn't believe him, and he got no help when a wolf did attack his flock. Although wolves rarely if ever attack humans——there is no documented case of such an attack in North America——much of their prey *is* lambs and calves. Thus this tale is familiar in almost every language. However, a Chinese version of it, one of the earliest, makes no mention of a wolf. It seems that the emperor Yu Wang of the third dynasty liked to amuse his favorite concubine by ringing alarm bells that warned his people that the enemy was approaching. His concubine always laughed when she saw people hurrying back into the walled city, but the people soon came to regard the bells as meaningless, and when the enemy really appeared the city was easily captured. Later tales—with wolves in them— may have derived from this one.

CUBBYHOLE

The *cub* or *cubby* in this term has nothing to do with bear cubs who live in a hole or den. *Cub* is a word still used in rural England for any small shelter, from a rabbit hutch to a chicken coop. Possibly first altered to *cubbyhole* by children in reference to a small hiding place, it came to mean any small, snug place.

CUCKOO

The *cuckoo,* instead of building its own nest, eats other birds' eggs and lays its eggs in their place. The cuckoo eggs are then hatched by the sparrow, wagtail, yellowhammer, or whatever. For this reason the bird's name became the basis for the derisive word *cuckold,* a husband whose wife has been unfaithful, a term that dates back more than a century before Chaucer's time. How cuckold came to be applied to the husband instead of the adulterer isn't clear, though Dr. Johnson believed that "it was usual to alarm the husband at the approach of an adultress by calling out 'Cuckoo,' which by mistake was applied in time to the person warned."

The cuckoo was so named for the one-note song it repeats over and over. Why it became a symbol for stupidity in the sixteenth century isn't really known. Perhaps it got this reputation because it lays its eggs in other birds' nests, though many would think this clever. Or we may owe that meaning of *cuckoo* to the folktale "Wise Men of Gotham," in which the villagers tried to prolong summer by fencing in the cuckoo so that it wouldn't fly off. (See also *Actaeon.*)

CUR

This word for a mean mongrel or worthless dog is associated with the snarling of such dogs. Used by Spenser in the *Faerie Queene, cur* is an old word that derives from the Scandinavian *kurra,* "to snarl or grumble."

CURRY FAVOR

These words are literally meaningless. What does *currying* or *brushing favor* have to do with bootlicking, or ingratiating oneself by flattery? The expression shows that a mistake repeated often enough can become standard usage. *Favor* here is a corruption of *Fauvel.* Fauvel was a fallow-colored or chestnut horse in the early-fourteenth-century satirical poem *Roman de Fauvel.* The equine hero of this popular French allegory symbolized cunning duplicity; thus cunning people who resorted to insincere flattery to gain someone's favor were said to *curry fauvel,* to groom or brush the rascally horse so that he would look kindly on them and perhaps impart to them his powers of duplicity. *Fauvel* came to be spelled *favel* in English. But because *favel* sounded like *favor* to Englishmen, and because the idea of gaining someone's favor is the essence of the phrase, the proverbial expression inevitably became to *curry favor*.

CYNIC

Disciples of the Greek philosopher Antisthenes (born c. 440 B.C.), especially his later followers like Diogenes, were nicknamed *kunikos* (cynikos), "doglike" or "snarlers," for their insolent, currish manners. Antisthenes and his pupils believed that independent virtue formed the sole basis for happiness, scorning freedom, honor, art, learning, health, riches—life itself. Insolently self-righteous, this small but influential band of ascetics derided all social customs, even sleeping in kennellike quarters. From their churlishness and rude manners we probably have our word *cynic,* meaning a surly, sarcastic person who believes that only selfishness motivates human behavior. It is possible, however, that this nickname was only a coincidence and that *cynic* derives from *Cynosarges* ("white dog"), the Greek gymnasium outside Athens where Antisthenes taught; or perhaps each word contributed to the other. (The gymnasium was supposedly named for a white dog that carried off part of a victim being offered to the gods.) But the Cynics outraged public standards of decency with their animallike philosophy and behavior. They lived without family, society, or religion, even adopting a dog as their common badge or symbol. The fact that Diogenes, a later Cynic, was nicknamed "the dog" may have also contributed to the coining.

DARK HORSE

A wonderful story is told about a swift, coal-black horse named Dusky Pete who belonged to Tennessean Sam Flyn. Sam made an easy living riding his horse from town to town and entering him in local races, which Dusty Pete, who looked like a lame plug, always won handily. But the story is fable as far as scholars are concerned. The phrase *dark horse* was first recorded in England, not America, in about 1830. Benjamin Disraeli used it in his *The Young Duke* (1831) as a racing term indicating more than the color of the horse: "A dark horse, which had never been thought of, rushed past the grand stand in sweeping triumph." Given Disraeli's widespread popularity as a novelist and public figure, it wasn't very long before the term was introduced in American politics to describe a candidate about whom little is known or who wins unexpectedly.

The Democratic convention of 1844 produced the first political dark horse in James Polk, who went on to become president, and the term was in wide use by 1865.

DAYMARE

On first coming across the word *daymare*, I thought it was a recent coinage by some whimsical writer. But *daymare*, patterned after *nightmare* and referring to a similar condition occurring during wakefulness, goes back to at least the early eighteenth century. It was probably invented by English author Matthew Green in his poem "The Spleen" (1737), which praised the simple contemplative life as a cure for boredom:

> The daymare Spleen,
> by whose false pleas
> men prove suicides in ease.

Coleridge confessed that he had daymares; an English medical writer called daymares "attacks of imperfect catalepsy," and James Russell Lowell implored:

> Help me to tame these wild day-mares
> That sudden on me unawares.

(See also *Nightmare, Incubus.*)

DEAD AS A DODO

The *dodo* left behind as its epitaph both its common name, which has become a synonym for stupidity and extinction, and its scientific name *Didus ineptus*, which says about the

69

same for it. By 1681, some 174 years after it was discovered by the Dutch on the islands of Reunion and Mauritius, east of Madagascar, the heavy, flightless bird became extinct. The dodo takes its name from the Portuguese *doudo*, "stupid." Dodos were not only big (larger than swans), very heavy, and flightless; they were also barely able to run. The colonists who settled the islands did not like their tough flesh, but the pigs, rats, and monkeys they brought with them found dodos and their eggs delicious. By the early eighteenth century gone was the short-winged bird that seemed "to have been invented for the sole purpose of becoming extinct," leaving behind only his sad story and a synonym for something or someone utterly extinct or hopelessly dumb.

THE DEATHWATCH

When the little beetle *Anobium tesellatum* clicked or tapped, according to an old superstition, death would come to someone in the house. The beetle was therefore named the deathwatch. Swift's poem *Wood an Insect* gives both the superstition and the antidote.

Chambermaids christen this worm a "Death-watch,"
Because like a watch, it always cries "click";
Then woe be to those in the house that are sick,
For sure as a gun they will give up the ghost . . .

But a kettle of scalding hot water injected
Infallibly cures the timber infected;
The omen is broken, the danger is over,
The maggot will die, and the sick will recover.

The sound of the deathwatch is really the beetle's mating call, which it makes by raising itself on its hind legs and beating its head rapidly against wood.

DEVIL'S ANIMALS

Thoreau and other New Englanders called the dragonfly the *devil's darning needle* and *devil's needle* because of its big eerie eyes, which are far out of proportion to its long, needlelike body. But the two colorful expressions yielded to the shorter *darning needle* over the years. Another colorful Americanism was *devil's riding horse* for the praying mantis. It was also called the *devil's horse, cheval du diable, devil's mare, devil's rear horse,* and *devil's war horse.* The praying mantis, or praying parson, took the name *mule killer* because someone confused it with the real mule killer, the whip-tailed scorpion.

DOG AND CAT NAMES

One man told me his wife named her dog after him, *before* they divorced, but there may be more bitterness in that than truth. On the other hand, H. L. Mencken, who [sic]ed himself on quite a few pompous "authorities," once confided that "several vicious hounds have been named Mencken" in America. There appears to be only one major study of the most popular names for dogs in this country, a radio contest sponsored in 1939 in which of 116,000 entries "1400 were named Prince, 1200 Queenie, 1000 Spot, 500 Rover and 30 each Tags, Towser, Muggsie, and Fido." Today, Lassie probably surpasses all these names, with Snoopy and other popular-culture hero names ranking high up there with the leaders.

One Thousand and One Names for Pets (1952) is a helpful book, but the number of names for pets in this country is probably at least ten times that many. Carolyn

Boyce Johnes's entertaining book *Please Don't Call Me Fido* presents many unusual names of dogs from history and fiction, including Bulova, for a watchdog; Seldom Fed, Underdog, Stop Damnit, Sir Love-a-Lot, Biter of Enemies, actress Joan Crawford's pups Gin and Tonic, Albert Einstein's poodle Chico, Albert Schweitzer's dog Choo Choo, and Bob Hope's German shepherd My Dog. She could not give the names for the wolfhound Columbus brought to America, the spaniel and mastiff that rode on the *Mayflower,* and the mutt that chased Paul Revere's horse. Neither did she mention Park Avenue pooches named Virginia Woof and Brigette Bar-dog—real names both.

There seem to be far fewer names for cats than dogs, perhaps because many people find cats too aloof and self-sufficient to get along with us on a first-name basis. People don't seem to play around with cat names, either. Has anyone heard of a real cat named Cheshire, or Kilkenny, or Nip, or Nap even? Tiger is a favorite name for cats, as are Tabitha and Piwackett, these last suggesting the occult with which the feline has long been associated. Probably the most ubiquitous cat name, aside from Tom or Puss, is Tabby (see *Tabby Cat*).

DOG DANCE

The *dog dance* was a ferocious dance of the Sioux Indian tribe that was held during the first full moon in each year. According to the observation of an American traveler in 1841: "The heart and liver of a dog are taken, raw and bleeding, and, cut into strips, placed on a stand about the height of a man's face from the ground; to this each of the warriors advance in turn, and, biting off a piece of the flesh, utters a yell of exultation."

DOG DAYS

Mad dogs don't give us our name for the hot, close days of July and August, though perhaps the prevalence of mad dogs at that time of year has kept the phrase *dog days* alive. The expression originated in Roman times as *caniculares dies,* days of the dog, and was an astronomical expression referring to the dog star Sirius or possibly Procyon. The Romans linked the rising of the Dog Star, the most brilliant star in the constellation Canis Major, with the sultry summer heat between about July 3 and August 11, believing that the star added to the extreme heat of the sun. Canicular days, of course, have nothing to do with heat from the Dog Star, but the ancient expression remains popular after over twenty centuries.

DOG ROSE

The wild, hardy dog rose (*Rosa canina,* called *cynorrodon* by Pliny) is said to have been so named because the Romans thought eating the flower cured the rabid bites of wild dogs. But then the Romans also believed that shortening a dog's tail was a preventative for rabies, and the Greeks thought dogs could cure many diseases by licking patients. The dissolute Greek warrior Alcibiades had a large, handsome dog with a beautiful tail that he cut off because he hoped doing so would make the Athenians talk about this eccentricity rather than his unscrupulous acts. Such stratagems of the "strategist" didn't work, for he was assassinated in 404 B.C., aged forty-six.

DOGMERD

British novelist Anthony Burgess apparently invented this word a few years ago, employing the English *dog* and the French *merde* (for excrement). It is a word more adult than all other euphemisms we have for good old Anglo-Saxon expressions, and yet it conveys the nose-squinching reaction one has stepping in the stuff.

DOGWOOD TREE

John C. Loudon wrote in his *The Hardy Trees and Shrubs of Britain* (1838) that the tree "is called Dogwood because a decoction of its leaves was used to wash dogs, to free them from vermin." This may be true, but no evidence has yet been found to support the theory. The beautiful ornamental (*Cornus florida*) was called the *dogges tree,* the *dogge berie tree,* the *hounder tree,* and the *hounde berie* tree as well as the *dogwood* in early times, so it surely has some connection with dogs. Another possibility is that it was named the *dogberry tree* because its dark purple berries resembled the berries of another, unknown tree that were used as a medicine for dogs, and that *dogberry* became *dogwood* in time. No link between the tree's wood and dogs has been found; we only know that in the past its wood was used to make toothpicks and that its crushed bark was thrown into the water to intoxicate fish and make them easy to catch by hand.

DON'T CHANGE HORSES IN
MIDSTREAM

The phrase, possibly suggested to Abraham Lincoln by an
old Dutch farmer he knew, is recorded almost a quarter of
a century before Lincoln said it. But Lincoln undoubtedly
made the words famous for all time when he accepted his
nomination for the presidency in 1864. Waving aside any
suggestions that the honor was a personal one, he told the
Republicans that he was sure they hadn't decided he was
"the greatest or the best man in America, but rather . . .
have concluded it is not best to swap horses while crossing
the river, and have further concluded that I am not so poor
a horse that they might not make a botch of it in trying to
swap." Over the years "the river," which was of course the
Civil War, was abbreviated to "midstream" and the saying
don't change horses in midstream came to mean "don't
change leaders in a crisis."

DON'T LOOK A GIFT HORSE
IN THE MOUTH

The age of a horse can be roughly determined by examining its teeth (see *Straight from the Horse's Mouth*). That
people knew this long before A.D. 400 is witnessed by the
appearance of the above expression in the writings of St.
Jerome, who called it a familiar proverb at the time. *Don't
look a gift horse in the mouth,* which means accept presents gracefully without trying to find something wrong with
them or determine how much they're worth, is literally re-
produced in German, French, and other languages, though

its first English use is *don't look a given horse in the mouth*. A variation on the phrase is *always look a gift horse in the mouth*—examine gifts closely, there may be strings attached. Cynical, but consider the Trojan horse.

DON'T STICK YOUR NECK OUT

Chickens, for some reason still known only to chickens, usually stretch out their necks when put on the chopping block, making it all the easier for the butcher to chop their heads off. Probably our expression warning someone not to expose himself to danger or criticism when this can be avoided, which is American slang from the late nineteenth century, originated from the bloody barnyard image. Lynchings have also been suggested, but men to be lynched rarely stick their necks out for the noose.

DORMOUSE

A member of the rodent family which the Romans raised for food, the little six-inch-long *dormouse* (*Glis glis*), resembles a small squirrel in looks and habits. Its name—about five centuries old—is something of a mystery, but many etymologists believe the creature is named for its appearance of sleepiness, that dormouse derives from the Swedish *dorsk*, "sleepy," or the Latin *dormire*, "to sleep." In fact, the dormouse, which Alice had such a hard time keeping awake at the Mad Hatter's tea party, is one of the legendary "seven sleepers" of the animal world, along with the ground squirrel, marmot, hedgehog, badger, bat, and bear. A hibernating dormouse—coiled up with its forefeet

76

tucked under its chin, its hind feet clenched in front of its face, and its tail curled over its face—can be rolled across a table like a wheel and won't come awake. The savage garden dormouse will immediately devour any dormouse that begins its winter sleep before the others, even its own mother.

DOVE'S DUNG

During a famine in Samaria, the Bible tells us (2 Kings 6:25) "an ass's head" was sold for fourscore pieces of silver and a quantity of "dove's dung" for five pieces of silver. This implies that dove's dung was eaten by the Samarians, surely one of the most disgusting substances ever used as food. It is said that the Hebrew for "lentils" and "locust pods" might easily be mistaken for "ass's head" and "dove's dung," but many modern versions of the Bible still translate the words as the latter. The expression might have been used for dramatic impact, but people have eaten some strange foods throughout history, including rats, cats, dogs, all manner of insects, and other people.

DRINK LIKE A FISH

Fish don't intentionally drink water, of course; they get whatever water they need from their food and most of the water they appear to be drinking while swimming along is actually passing through their gills to supply them with oxygen. But they certainly do *seem* to be drinking continuously, many swimming with their mouths open, and that is why *drink like a fish* has been a common synonym for drinking excessively, especially alcohol, since at least the early seventeenth century.

DUPE

Because its cry sounds like "up up" the south European bird *Upupa epops* was called the *upup* or *upupa* by the Romans. The bird, about the size of a large thrush and noted for its long, curved beak, variegated plumage, and the male's beautiful orange erectile crest, became known in French as the *huppe* and in English as the *hoopoe* or *hoop*. But the French considered it to be an especially stupid bird, perhaps because it laid its eggs most anywhere without a nest (in a hole in a wall, tree, or bank), perhaps because the insect feeder "is filthy in food and habits." Anyway, Frenchmen commonly said that any fool had the head of a *huppe*, a *tête d'uppe*. Eventually the *d'uppe* in the expression became *duppe* and passed into English as *dupe*, a person who is easily fooled or deceived.

EAGER BEAVER

You'd think that this expression would have been around
for centuries, referring as it does to industrious beavers
gnawing away on and felling trees, swimming back and
forth from their construction sites all day carrying sticks
and mud for their dams and houses. But *eager beaver*
comes from the Canadian army and isn't recorded before
1940, although it obviously derives from such phrases as
busy as a beaver, which dates back to the early eighteenth
century. Unlike the early expression, however, *eager beaver* is usually applied derisively to someone who is overly
industrious in his work, one who tries to impress his superi-
ors by his diligence and becomes obnoxious to his associ-
ates as a result.

EARMARK

Back in the sixteenth century English farmers began to notch their own identifying marks in the ears of their sheep and cattle to prevent them from being stolen. This practice didn't always work, for many thieves were adept at altering *earmarks,* but the animal earmark was so common that it soon gave its name to any kind of identifying mark, and, figuratively, to something marked or set aside for some special purpose—such as money earmarked for a particular purpose. Incidentally, thieves who altered an earmark ran the risk of being sent to prison where they themselves would be earmarked. Slitting the ears of pilloried criminals, earmarking them, was as common as nose slitting or earmarking animals in those days.

EARWIG

The nocturnal *earwig* (*Forficula auricularia*) is a common garden pest, but it won't wiggle or wriggle into people's ears and then drill its way into the brain with the aid of its large pincers. Yet it was exactly this popular superstition that gave the earwig or *earwiggle* its name over a thousand years ago. One English writer even instructed: "If an earwig begotten into your eare . . . spit into the same, and it will come forth anon." Good trick if you can do it.

To earwig someone is to fill his mind with prejudices by insinuations, by whispering into his ear and wriggling into his confidence.

EASEL

The three-legged frame used to hold a painting while the artist works on it suggested a donkey to seventeenth-century Dutch painters because it somewhat resembled one and because it carried a burden. So they named this piece of equipment an *ezel,* Dutch for donkey, the word changing to *easel* in English as use of the device increased. The idea seems to be a widespread one, however, as the French call an *easel* a *chevalet,* a wooden "horse."

TO EAT CROW

During an armistice toward the end of the War of 1812, an American soldier out hunting crossed the Niagara River past British lines. Finding no better game, he shot a crow, but a British officer heard the shot and surprised him. The Britisher tricked the Yankee out of his rifle by praising his marksmanship and asking if he could inspect the rifle with which the Yankee shot so well. He then turned the gun on the American, demanding that he take a bite out of the crow he had shot as a punishment for violating British territory. The American complied, but when the officer returned his weapon and told him to leave, the Yankee covered the Englishman and forced him to eat the rest of the crow. That is the origin of the expression *to eat crow,* to be forced to do something extremely disagreeable, as related in an 1888 issue of the Atlanta *Constitution.* Although to eat crow is possibly a much older expression, the saying first appeared in print in 1877 and the story may well be true—nothing better has been suggested. The concept behind to eat crow is that crows are not good eating, but the flesh of young ones was once esteemed, and I have it on the authority of the Remington Arms Co. that even old crows aren't so bad if you simply: "skin the bird, salt and cut it into pieces, parboil till tender and then fry with butter and onions."

TO EAT HUMBLE PIE

Here is an expression probably born as a pun. The *humble* in this pie has nothing to do etymologically with the word *humble*, "lowly," which is from the Latin *humilis*, "low or slight." Umbles or numbles (from the Latin *lumbulus*, "little loin") were the innards—the heart, liver, and entrails—of deer and were often made into a pie. Sir Walter Scott called this dish "the best" and an old recipe for it (1475) instructed "For to serve a Lord"—but some thought it fit only for servants. When the lord of a manor and his guests dined on venison, the menials ate umble pie made from the innards of the deer. Anyone who ate umble pie was therefore in a position of inferiority—he or she was humbled—and some anonymous punster in the time of William the Conqueror, realizing this, changed *umble pie* to *humble pie*, the pun all the more effective because in several British dialects, especially the Cockney, the *h* is silent and *humble* is pronounced *umble* anyway. So the play upon words gave us the common expression *to eat humble pie*, to suffer humiliation, to apologize, or to abase oneself profoundly.

ELEPHANTINE AND
OTHER ANIMAL CLICHÉS

Elephantine has been used too often recently to describe not someone immense but someone slow and clumsy. As Bil Gilbert points out in his article "Fast as an Elephant, Strong as an Ant" (*Sports Illustrated*, April 25, 1966), both in the wild and in captivity elephants are extremely graceful beasts that can run up to twenty-five miles an hour. *"Horsine,"* he writes, "would be a better term to designate a stumblebum. Horses are forever falling over small pebbles, ropes and their own feet." Mr. Gilbert examines a menagerie of animal clichés in his article, including *loose as a goose* ("geese have rigid pinions and are more or less bound like weight lifters by a heavy layer of pectoral muscle"), *quick as a cat, strong as an ox, runs like a rabbit, wolfish grin,* and *wild as a hawk.* He offers some interesting and more accurate substitutions, such as *wild as a heron, loose as a mink,* and *baboon-quick.*

EPIZOOTIC

Deriving from the Greek *epi,* "upon or among," and *zoo,* "animal," this is the animal counterpart for the *epidemics* that affect people. *Epizootic* diseases include rabies and hoof-and-mouth disease. The Great Epizootic (the word can be both noun and adjective) of 1872 claimed almost a quarter of the nation's horses (some four million) and left America without the power it needed to function for three months—most power at the time being horse power. Scientists never isolated the virus that caused the epizootic, and it only ended its ravages when cold weather killed the

83

mosquitoes that transmitted the deadly virus. By that time the financial losses suffered had helped bring on the Panic of 1873. To a nation wholly dependent on horse power, the epizootic was indeed a tragedy. In cities across the country homes went without heat, fires blazed unfought, garbage wasn't collected, deliveries were halted, public transportation ceased, stores closed, and unemployment soared. Racetracks closed their gates and at least one great American thoroughbred, Pocahontas, fell to the disease. In several cities unemployed men were even harnessed to carts and trolleys, pulling them down the street in place of horses.

EVERY DOG HAS HIS DAY

Cervantes apparently deserves credit for this proverb, which is given in *Don Quixote* (1605–1615). Two centuries later, English author George Barrow wrote: "Youth will be served, every dog has his day, and mine has been a fine one." No one has been able to trace the proverb to the Himalayan valleys north of India, where all dogs literally do have a day. Dog's Day in the region is called *Khich mavas* by the Kashmiris and *Swana Boli* by the Nepalese. It is a day when humans pay reverence to dogs as their brothers and sisters among living things. Choice food is set out for the dogs; even the mangiest strays get flower garlands hung around their necks and the Nepalese dogs wear the red spot of Hindu holiness imprinted on their foreheads. The following day things get back to normal until the next Dog's Day and the dogs lead a dog's life, 364 days of curses, kicks, and stonings from humans who consider them unclean and contemptible.

FAUNA

Linnaeus coined this term for all the animals of a given place in a given time, first using it in the title of his *Fauna Suecica* (1745) and taking the name *fauna* from the Roman rural goddess. Fauna, like her brother Faunus, was a prophetic woodland deity who guarded the herds and gave fertility to them.

A FEATHER IN YOUR CAP

Few people today consider it honorable to kill their enemies and keep count, though nightly television news programs during the Vietnam War flashed accounts of

American and Vietcong dead across the screen like basketball scores. But the expression *a feather in your cap,* an honor, is in allusion to the custom many peoples have had of adding feathers to their headdress for every enemy they killed. The saying is recorded as early as 1655; the custom is much older and almost universal. The ancient Lycians, Hungarians, Turks, Chinese, Abyssinians, Himalayan tribesmen, and American Indians all practiced it in one form or another. Possibly the expression was strengthened by the crest of three ostrich feathers awarded to sixteen-year-old Edward "the Black Prince," son of Edward III, for his valor at the Battle of Crécy in 1346. This crest of John, King of Bohemia, became the badge of each succeeding Prince of Wales. Another strengthening factor is the ancient custom of a hunter plucking a feather from the first bird on opening day of the hunting season and sticking it in his cap. American gunfighters, not to be outdone by the Indians with their feathers, carved notches on their guns for each kill, giving us the roughly equivalent phrase *a notch on his gun.*

FEEL ONE'S OATS

Someone *feeling his oats* or *full of oats* is in high spirits, full of pep, so full of self that he may even be showing off a bit. The allusion is to the fact that horses fed on oats become lively, and the expression is American, first recorded in 1843 by Canadian humorist Thomas Haliburton. Men, women, and children can feel their oats, but only young men are said to *sow* their wild oats.

FEISTY

A *feist,* first spelled *foist, fice,* or *fise,* was in George Washington's time a little, ill-natured cur full of fight. An Americanism, the term probably has its roots in the British *fysting curre* and *fisting hound,* which date back to the sixteenth century and have their origins in the word *fist.* Americans used *feist* for any small, ill-tempered mongrel, and by the early twentieth century this name for a combative dog became the adjective *feisty,* belligerent, high-spirited, and fidgety. (See also *Cur.*)

TO FIGHT LIKE KILKENNY CATS

> There once were two cats of Kilkenny,
> Each thought there was one cat too many;
> So they fought and they fit
> And they scratched and they bit,
> Till excepting their nails
> And the tips of their tails,
> Instead of two cats there weren't any.
> —Traditional

During the Irish rebellion or revolution of 1798, Hessian mercenaries stationed in Kilkenny amused themselves by tying two cats by their tails and throwing them over a clothing line to fight to the death. Just before an officer interrupted their banned "sport" unexpectedly one day, a quick-thinking trooper cut off the two tails and let the cats escape, telling the colonel that the soldiers had nothing to do with the fight—the two cats had just devoured each other except for the tails.

The above tale may have inspired the expression *to fight*

like Kilkenny cats, to fight bitterly until the end, and indeed these Kilkenny cats are pictured in Hogarth's *Four Stages of Cruelty.* But another story has it that two Kilkenny cats fought so ferociously in a sandpit that they devoured each other except for their tails. And still another yarn has a thousand fabled Kilkenny cats fighting an all-night battle with a thousand cats selected by "sportsmen" from all over Ireland, the tough Kilkenny cats killing them all. Unfortunately, most authorities go along with Jonathan Swift, more conservative, who prefers the explanation that *cats* in the phrase refers to men. It seems that in the seventeenth century residents of Englishtown and Irishtown in Kilkenny—which was cut in half by a stream—were constantly fighting over boundary lines and were compared to battling cats. But nobody has offered convincing proof for any one of these stories.

A FINE KETTLE OF FISH

Brewer and many others claim that this expression of disgust for an awful mess (also *a pretty* or *nice kettle of fish*) has its origins in a kind of picnic held along the river Tweed in the eighteenth century, the picnic called "a kettle of fish" because salmon from the river were boiled in kettles and served to the guests, who ate them under marquees on the riverbank. The reasoning is that the fish were often overcooked, undercooked, or seasoned improperly, that the kettle of fish frequently spilled over, or that eating the fish was messy—any or all of these situations giving rise to our term for a mess, or muddle. These *fêtes champêtres* or kettles of fish *were* held, but that is the only evidence linking them to the expression. Just as good an explanation is found in the English word *kiddle.* A *kiddle* or *kiddle net* is a basket set in the sluiceways of dams to catch fish, a device well known from the time of the Plantagenets. Royal officials often had the perquisite to trap fish in kiddles, but poachers sometimes raided the traps for fish, frequently destroying the kiddles in the process. Possibly an official came upon a destroyed trap and exclaimed, "That's a pretty kiddle of fish!" or something similar, meaning "a pretty sorry state of affairs!" and the phrase was born. Repeated over the years *kiddle* was corrupted in everyday speech to *kettle*, giving us the expression as we know it today.

A FISH OUT OF WATER

Older by at least several hundred years than the dates cited in the *OED* and the *Oxford Dictionary of Quotations*, this expression may even have originated with the Greek patriarch St. Athanasius of the fourth century. Its earliest recorded use, however, is by English theologian and religious reformer John Wycliffe in his *English Works* (c. 1380): "And how thei weren out of ther cloistre as fish is withouten water." The metaphor, as widely used as ever today, describes anyone floundering in an element or environment to which he is unaccustomed and in which he is practically helpless.

FLAMINGO

The long-legged, pink wading bird, depicted in prehistoric man's cave drawings, was named by Spanish explorers in the New World for the people of Flanders, the Flemings, as they were called. These people were widely known for their lively personalities, flushed complexions, and love of bright, gay clothing. The Spaniards thought it was a great joke, naming the bird the *flamenco*, which means "a Fleming" and became the English *flamingo* in time. In fact, they liked the joke so much that they also named their lively dance the *flamenco* after the lively Flemings.

TO FLOG (OR BEAT)
A DEAD HORSE

Though he supported the measure, British politician and orator John Bright thought the Reform Bill of 1867, granting more democratic representation, would never be passed by Parliament. Trying to rouse Parliament from its apathy on the issue, he said in a speech, would be like trying *to flog a dead horse* to make it pull a load. This is the first recorded use of the expression, which is still common for trying to revive interest in an apparently hopeless issue. Bright's silver tongue is also responsible for "England is the mother of Parliaments," and "Force is not a remedy," among other memorable quotations.

A FLY IN THE OINTMENT

"Dead flies cause the ointment of the apothecary to send forth a stinking savour; so doth a little folly him that is in reputation for wisdom and honour." The unknown author of the Biblical book of Ecclesiastes (a Greek rendering of the Hebrew word *Koheleth,* preacher) wrote these words in the third century B.C. Like many other vivid figures of speech in the twenty-first book of the Old Testament ("Vanity of vanities, saith the preacher . . . all is vanity,"

"For everything there is a season," "He who digs a pit will fall into it"), these words from the first verse of the tenth chapter became proverbial when translated into English. For five centuries now *a fly in the ointment* has meant a small defect that spoils something valuable or is a source of annoyance.

G

In the old Phoenician alphabet *G* represented the outline of a camel's head and neck.

TO GET A RISE
OUT OF SOMEONE

When these words were first used they applied to fish rising to the bait. Izaak Walton and other writers on the art of angling popularized the word *rise* in this sense three hundred years ago, and the metaphor from fly-fishing became standard English. Just as the fish rises to the bait and is caught, the person who rises to the lure of a practical joke becomes the butt of it. From its original meaning of raising a laugh at someone's expense, the words have been extended to include the idea of attracting attention in general—getting a rise out of a sales prospect, for example.

TO GET ONE'S BACK UP

No one knows exactly when the aggressive arching of an angry cat's back suggested these words for humans aroused into anger, but it's surprising that the phrase *to get one's back up* is no more than two centuries old, for an angry cat with its back arched high when attacked by a dog or other animal is an impressive sight and a common one wherever there are felines wild or domestic. Cats were introduced to Europe long before the Crusades and became valued pets, despite their aloofness, when they demonstrated a proficiency at rat killing at least equal to the ferret's and proved far more prolific and easier to keep.

TO GET ONE'S GOAT

High-strung race horses often have goats as stable mates on the theory that the goats have a calming effect on the thoroughbreds. But the horses grow attached to their companions and become upset if they are removed, throwing off their performance on the track. It's said that nineteenth-century gamblers capitalized on this fact by stealing the goat of a horse they wanted to lose the next day and that this practice gave us the phrase *to get one's goat*—they got the horse's goat and he became upset or angry. It's as good an explanation as any, but isn't supported by much evidence. Jack London was the first to record the expression in his novel *Smoke Bellew* (1912), and though its usage there has nothing to do with racing, London was certainly familiar with underworld practices. Attempts have also been made to connect the goat in the phrase with the scapegoat of Hebrew tradition, with the word *goad,* "to anger or irritate," and to an old French phrase *prendre la chèvre,* literally meaning "to take the goat," which dates back to the sixteenth century and certainly took a long time making the journey to America if it is the source of our expression.

TO GET UP
ON ONE'S HIGH HORSE

In the royal pageants of medieval England nobles and others of high rank customarily rode "high horses," great chargers a hand or so taller than the average mount. Riding such a high horse naturally came to be equated with superiority and the arrogance superiority often breeds. *To ride the high horse* came to mean to affect arrogance or superiority, and this phrase gave us the still common *to get up on one's high horse,* to scorn what we consider "beneath us."

GIBBON

Is this long-armed ape really named after a man? Possibly, if it's true that the naming was the practical joke of an eminent naturalist. Several respected etymologists believe that this is the case. Apparently the French naturalist Buffon first named the Indian ape in his *Natural History* (1749–1804). The witty Buffon may have been aware that the tombs of the English Gybbon family in Kent, "dating from about 1700, are surmounted by an ape's head, the family crest." A less inspired derivation suggests that *gibbon* comes from an Indian dialect, but there is no abundant evidence for either theory. The smallest of the apes, the gibbon is often kept as a household pet by Malaysians.

GIT ALONG, LITTLE DOGIE

The dogie in the song is a motherless calf. Such undernourished calves often have distended sagging bellies, which may have reminded cowboys of a batch of sourdough the chuck wagon cook carried in a sack. From this association the calves may have been called *doughbellies*, then *doughies* and finally *dogies*. The origin of the word really hasn't been established. No one seems to believe that the calves were called dogies because they were so undernourished that, compared to healthy calves, they resembled dogs.

GIVE A WHALING TO

Many etymologists believe this phrase should be *give a waling to,* as a *wale* is a mark raised on the flesh by the blow of a stick or whip. But the key word in the phrase has been spelt with an *h* ever since it first appeared two centuries ago, which suggests that a *whaling*, a terrible beating, was one given with a whalebone whip, or, possibly, that the whalebone whip and the wales it raised both contributed to the phrase, making it more vivid. Riding whips were commonly made of whalebone in the eighteenth and nineteenth centuries and used to beat more than horses. Whalebone, incidentally, is a misnomer—it's not from the bones of a whale but from baleen, a substance found in the whale's upper jaw.

TO GO HOG WILD

The phrase *to go hog wild* means to become wildly excited or irrational from excitement, anger, or even happiness. The Americanism probably originated in the mid-nineteenth century, though it isn't recorded until about fifty years later. It obviously refers to the way hogs become wildly excited when aroused and is just as obviously another phrase from the farm, still hanging in there long after most Americans began buying their bacon wrapped in cellophane.

TO GO TO THE DOGS, TO LEAD A DOG'S LIFE

Dogs aren't the prized, often pampered, pets in other countries that they are in America. In the East they are often considered pariahs and scavengers of the streets, and the Chinese, Koreans, and Japanese, among other Asians, commonly eat them. Englishmen of earlier times used dogs primarily for hunting and kept them outside or in a rude shelter, not generally as house pets. The dogs were fed table scraps and these they had to fight over. It didn't seem much fun, a dog's life, and Englishmen of the sixteenth century began to compare anyone who had become impoverished, who was going to utter ruin naturally or morally, with their maltreated canines. *To lead a dog's life* was to be bothered every moment, never to be left in peace; *to go to the dogs* was to become just like the helpless animals; and *to die like a dog* was to come to a miserable, shameful end. There were many other similar phrases that arose before the dogs had their day in England and America: *throw it to the dogs*, to throw something away that's worthless; and, of course, *a dirty dog*, a morally reprehensible or filthy person. (See also *Hangdog Look; In the Dog-house*.)

TO GO WHOLE HOG

Probably the expression *to go the whole hog*, or *to go whole hog*, to go the limit, all the way, has its origins in William Cowper's poem "The Love of the World Reproved; or Hypocrisy Detected" (1779). Cowper told a story about pious but hungry Mohammedans who were ordered by Mohammed not to eat a certain unspecified part of the pig. Unable to determine what part, they began to experiment:

> But for one piece they thought it hard
> From the whole hog to be debar'd;
> And set their wit at work to find
> What joint the prophet had in mind . . .
> Thus, conscience freed from every clog,
> Mohometans eat up the hog . . .
> With sophistry their sauce they sweeten,
> Til quite from tail to snout 'tis eaten.

The words *whole hog* and the idea of going whole hog are in the poem, but other writers have different ideas about the expression's origins. One links it with the Irish

97

nickname "hog" for a shilling—parsimonious Irishmen in bars were urged to go the whole hog (spend the whole shilling) on drink. Another theory says that the hog in the phrase was originally a sheep, not a hog. Young sheep were called hogs and had to be clipped very carefully because they hadn't been shorn before. Workers were warned not to be careless, to clip the whole animal or go the whole hog, do the job thoroughly.

GOATEE

The style of chin whiskers cut in the form of a tuft like that of a he-goat apparently became popular in mid-nineteenth-century America, when the word *goatee* is first recorded. Goatee simply means "little goat" and the Americanism is first recorded in 1842 as *goaty*. In his novel *Major Jones's Courtship* (1843), William Tappan Thompson has a character describe a goatee this way: "One chap's jist come from the north, rigged out like a show monkey, with a little tag of hair hangin down under his chin jist like our old billy goat, that's a leetle too smart for this latitude, I think." *Billygoat beard* or *whiskers* means the same and is first recorded in the mid-1880s.

GOATSUCKER

This nocturnal bird (*Caprimulgus europaeus*), also known as the nightjar because its calls "jar the night," is called the *goatsucker* in Greek, Latin, French, German, Spanish, and several other languages besides English, its name reflecting the widespread belief that it attacks and sucks the udders of goats for food. Aristotle was among the first to note the legend, writing that "flying to the udders of she goats, it sucked them and so it gets its name. They say that the udder withers when it has sucked it and that the goat goes blind." Even this bird's scientific name *Caprimulgus* honors the story, deriving from the Latin *caper*, "goat," and *mulgere*, "to milk." The short-billed, wide-mouthed bird actually feeds on insects it captures in the air. The goatsucker family consists of sixty-seven members, including the poor will, the only bird that hibernates, and the whippoorwill. The whippoorwill was named for its cry, which the naturalist John Burroughs once heard 1,478 times in succession from a single bird. The eerie voices of whippoorwills are said to be the voices of the restless souls of dead criminals and in Appalachia the whippoorwill's cry supposedly tells the unmarried years left to a bachelor.

GOD TEMPERS THE WIND TO THE SHORN LAMB

Since lambs are never shorn, Laurence Sterne's phrase, from his *Sentimental Journey* (1768), seems to make little sense. Sterne coined it from an earlier, less poetic expression—invented some one hundred and forty years before—that said, *To a close-shorn sheep, God gives wind by measure.* But George Herbert, the author of this, got it in turn from a French saying in Henri Estienne's *Premices* (1594) which said *God regulates the cold to the shorn lamb.* Poetry usually triumphs.

GOING BY SHANK'S MARE

Going by shank's mare means going somewhere by walking, using Walker's bus, and as far as is known no horseless Mr. Shank is responsible for the two-hundred-year-old phrase, which is probably Scottish in origin. Neither is there any proof that the expression refers to King Edward I, nicknamed "Longshanks" because whenever he rode a pony his long legs reached to the ground. The *shank* is the leg, or that part of the leg below the knee, and a mare is usually slower than a stallion, its pace closer to a walk. Going by Marrow-bone stage, a play on the once real Marylebone (pronounced "Marrybun") stage or coach in London, means the same.

A GONE GOOSE

No connection has been made between this American expression and the much older phrase *cook your goose* (*q.v.*). Apparently, the Americanism only dates from about 1830, and there is no story about a goose in a helpless, hopeless state to explain it. Probably *a gone goose, a gone beaver, a gone chick,* and similar expressions all derive from the earlier *a gone coon,* which, according to one of several legends, goes back to the Revolutionary War. It seems that an American had disguised himself in raccoon skins and climbed a tree to spy on the British. But an enemy soldier discovered him that night while coon hunting and took aim, ready to shoot the biggest coon he had ever seen, when the spy cried out, "Don't shoot—I'll come down! I know I'm a gone coon!" According to the legend, the British soldier was so terrified to hear an "animal" talk that he dropped his gun and ran. The tale need not be true for it to have popularized the expression *a gone coon* and other animals could have been substituted for the coon by storytellers in different areas of the country. Later the coon story was changed and told about many famous marksmen. Davy Crockett, for example, was supposed to have treed a raccoon that pleaded, "Don't shoot, I'll come down, I know I'm a gone coon."

TO GOOSE

Mencken characterized *to goose* as "one of the most mysterious of American verbs." No other language employs this term for "to jab sharply with the thumb in the anus, with the intention of startling or stimulating," which is only about sixty years old and has taken on the additional meaning of goading someone into action. There are many theories about the word's etymology. Most experts lean to Partridge's explanation that pugnacious geese "sometimes attack human beings, and especially children, by biting their fundaments." Since they are also said "to attack women by striking at the pudenda," the sexual associations are obvious. Others say that goose breeders examine their birds' rear parts for eggs before turning them out from the pens each day and that thrusts of a similar nature are the only way to distinguish between male and female geese in certain varieties—either practice could have inspired the expression. *To goose* could also be a euphemism for *to roger,* eighteenth-century British slang for "to have sexual intercourse," since Roger, like Dobbin for a horse, was a conventional English folk name for a goose. Finally, there is the suggestion that to goose is named from a poolroom receptacle called "the goose" that "grab-ass" jokers frequently jabbed into the fundament of a pool player just as he was about to make a shot.

GOOSE PIMPLES

When geese are plucked, the thousands of tiny muscles that pull their feathers erect to form a natural insulation system continue to contract in the cold. The contracted muscles look like bumpy, pimply skin on a bare bird and as far back as the seventeenth century suggested the bumps on human skin caused by cold or fear. At first this condition was called *goose flesh* or *goose skin*, or "creeping of the flesh." A fancier name is *horripilation*, "erection of the hair on the skin by contraction of the cutaneous muscles caused by cold, fear or other emotion." This word effectively suggests fear and derives from the Latin *horrere*, to bristle or shudder, which gives us the word *horror*.

GOPHER

Probably theatrical in origin and dating back to the 1940s *gopher*, also spelled *gofer*, is a corruption of the words *go for*. It describes an errand person, hired to do menial chores—to "go for" coffee and doughnuts or whatever else the boss and other higher-ups can't acquire from a sedentary position.

A gopher can also be a zealous salesman, in this case the "go for" deriving from "go for broke."

Earlier a gopher or gopher man was a miner who, by using explosives, burrowed into the earth, this name transferred to a safe blower or safecracker at the turn of the

102

century. Here the source for gopher is the burrowing animal, which takes its name from the French *gaufre*, "honeycomb," in reference to the animal's burrow.

TO GRIN LIKE A
CHESHIRE CAT

The pseudonymous British satirist Peter Pindar (John Wolcot) first used this expression for a broad smile in the late eighteenth century, but Lewis Carroll popularized it in *Alice's Adventures in Wonderland* (1865). The Cheshire cat in the story gradually faded from Alice's view, its grin the last part of it to vanish. No satisfactory explanation of the allusion has been made. *To grin like a Cheshire cat* probably goes back much further than Pindar, and the source could be Cheshire cheeses, which were at one time molded in the form of a cat—supposedly, the cat was grinning because the former palatine of Cheshire once had regal privileges in England, paying no taxes to the crown. Another story relates the expression to the attempts of an ignorant sign painter to represent a lion rampant on the signs of many Cheshire inns—his lions looked more like grinning cats. The most unlikely yarn credits an eponymous forest warden of Cheshire named Caterling. In the reign of Richard III, it's said, this Cheshire Caterling stamped out poaching, was responsible for over one hundred poachers being hanged, and was present "grinning from ear to ear" at each of these executions. *To grin like a Cheshire Catling* became proverbial and was later shortened to *to grin like a Cheshire cat*. Another fanciful story makes the same Mr. Catling the cat of the nursery rhyme "Hey Diddle Diddle, the Cat and the Fiddle." There is no record of him.

GROUNDHOG

American settlers named the marmot or woodchuck *(Arctomys monax)* the groundhog, perhaps because this member of the squirrel family seems hoggish in the way he burrows through the ground. Or, possibly, groundhog is a translation of the Dutch *aardvark* made by Dutch settlers in America, even though the South African aardvark or earth hog is a larger burrowing animal than the groundhog. The groundhog isn't a hog then, but his other American name, woodchuck, is no more accurate, for he doesn't chuck wood, either, a fact even the old tongue twister implies: "How much wood would a woodchuck chuck if a woodchuck could chuck wood?" Woodchuck has no connection with wood at all, simply deriving from the Cree Indian word *wuchuk* or *otcheck* for another animal, the fisher or pekan, which early settlers corrupted finally to woodchuck and applied through mistaken identity to the groundhog.

Groundhog Day, February 2, is the day when the groundhog is supposed to emerge from his hibernation, look outside, and go back to bed again if he sees his shadow, in anticipation of more severe weather unfit for man or groundhog. The custom is American, but has been linked to a British superstition about Candlemas Day, February 2, which is best illustrated by this old proverb first recorded in 1612: "If Candlemas day be fair and bright, winter will have another flight: If on Candlemas day be shower and rain, winter is gone, and will not come again."

Candlemas Day is the feast of the Purification of the Virgin Mary, the day so named because all the candles used in Catholic churches during the year are consecrated at this time. There are several other weather superstitions relating to Candlemas Day, including the following one from an old German proverb: "The badger peeps out of his hole on Candlemas Day, and if he finds snow, walks abroad; but if he sees the sun shining he draws back into his hole."

GUINEA PIG

The South American rodent isn't a pig, doesn't look like a pig, and doesn't hail from Guinea in West Africa. Native to Brazil, where it has long been raised for food, it takes its first name from the fact that it was originally brought to Europe on the Guinea-men slave ships that sailed from Guinea to South America to deliver their human cargo and filled their holds with whatever cargo was available for the trip back across the ocean to Europe. How the creature was mistaken for a pig is anybody's guess. Our slang expression *guinea pig,* for anyone on whom something is tested, obviously derives from the widespread use of the guinea pig in scientific experiments. A better name for the guinea pig is cavy, but few people use it.

GULL

The *gull,* the only bird ever to have a monument erected to it, is intimately connected with English and American history. All gulls take their name from Breton *gwylan* for the bird, which derives from the Breton *gwela,* to weep, in reference to the bird's cry. *Franklin's gull* was named in honor of Sir John Franklin (1786–1847), the English explorer who died in discovering the Northwest Passage that so many other mariners had striven to find. The story of his expedition and his wife's later attempts to find him is one of the most interesting in maritime history. But Franklin's gull (*Larus pipixan*), which has the same upland-breeding and seashore-wintering habits as the Bonaparte gull, isn't as prominent in American folklore as the California gull (*Larus californicus*). In 1848 an invasion of grasshoppers threatened starvation for the Mormon settlers near the Great Salt Lake and it was checked only by the appearance of flocks of California gulls that devoured the crickets and saved the crops after all other means had failed. "I heard the voice of fowels flying overhead . . . and saw a flock of seven gulls," wrote a Mormon pioneer. "They came faster and more of them until the heavens were darkened with them and they would eat crickets. . . . In the morning they came back again and continued that course until they had devoured the crickets." The Sea Gull Monument on Temple Square in Salt Lake City is dedicated to the species, "in grateful remembrance of the mercy of God to the Mormon pioneers." In a similar incident in 1947 black-headed gulls destroyed a plague of caterpillars in Scotland.

To gull, or to deceive someone, and the word *gullible* possibly derive from a reference to the gull voraciously feeding (as it does) and swallowing everything (hook, line, and sinker!), suggesting that someone can be fed lies.

GUPPY

By far the best known and most popular of home aquarium fish, aside from the goldfish, is the *guppy* or rainbow fish (*lebistes reticulatus,* also called the millions fish). Guppies take their name from R. J. Lechmere Guppy, president of the Scientific Association of Trinidad, who presented the British Museum with specimens of the species in the late nineteenth century. Since then many handsome exotic types have been developed. In courtship the smaller males (one inch long) are particularly interesting, fanning out their colorful tails to attract the females. Guppies bear their young live, giving birth to from an average of 50 to as many as 185 babies at a time and bearing offspring every four weeks. Abundant in South America, the fish devour mosquito larvae and so help to prevent malaria. They have also proved useful in genetic experiments.

The streamlined *guppy submarine* developed toward the end of World War II is named for the guppy, but its name is also an acronym, the first four letters standing for "greater underwater propulsion power." The guppy was twice as fast as any old-style sub. (See also *Molly.*)

THE HAIR OF
THE DOG THAT BIT YOU

Like cures like, *similia similibus curantur,* the Romans believed, like many ancient people before them, and they commonly bound hairs of a dog that had bitten someone to that person's wound in order to make it heal better—even if the dog was rabid. The treatment was recommended for centuries by serious medical books, about the only change until medieval times being that *burnt* hair of the dog that bit you was prescribed. By then it was also believed that the best cure for a hangover was a drink of the same poison that stifflicated you the night before and the old proverb *a hair of the dog that bit you* applied to this practice. The first mention of the phrase in reference to hangovers is in John Heywood's *Proverbs* (1546): "I pray thee leat me and

108

my felow have a heare of the dog that bote us last night—
and bitten were we both to the braine aright." Today virtually no one puts dog's hair on dog bites, but a hair of the
dog that bit you is still a universal "remedy" for a hangover. The practice makes some sense, too, for alcohol se-
dates those rebounding nerves that make hangovers so
acutely painful.

HAIRY

Hairy as slang for unpleasant or rough seems to be of
Army origin, from about 1935, when a *hairy patrol* was an
unpleasant one that met with resistance. Its origin is unknown, but the word may have something to do with *to
make one's hair stand on end* (*q.v.*) and *scary.* Another
possibility, a long shot, is the English expression *hairy at
the heel,* common in the late nineteenth century. A horse
with hair about the heels or fetlocks was an underbred one,
so the expression was used figuratively for an ill-bred, bad-
mannered, thoroughly unpleasant person, as was hairy.

HALCYON DAYS

When a storm shipwrecked and killed her mortal husband,
the heartbroken Alcyone, daughter of Aeolus, the wind
god of Greek legend, drowned herself in the sea. The gods,
punishing the suicide, turned both Alcyone and her husband into birds later known as *halcyons,* or kingfishers as
we call them today. But her father took pity on the couple
and decreed that during the halcyon's breeding season, the
seven days before and the seven days after the shortest day
of the year, the sea would always be perfectly calm and un-

ruffled. Thus, during the fourteen days at about the time of the winter solstice, the halcyons could sit on their nests hatching their eggs as the spongelike masses floated securely on the tranquil water, borne by currents across the world. This legend was widely believed through Roman times, when Alcyone's name became Halcyon, and well into the fifteenth century. The halcyon days had an actual place on ancient calendars, and the legend inspired much poetry, including Shelley's famous:

> The halcyons brood around the foamless isles,
> The treacherous ocean has forsworn its wiles.

Kingfishers were also believed to be able to predict the weather, and stuffed specimens, wings outstretched, were even used as weather vanes. Eventually, all the legends and the exquisitely peaceful sound of the word *halcyon* (pronounced hal-see-un) itself made the phrase *halcyon days* mean not only windless days of peace and calm but any time of peace, serenity, and rejoicing.

HALIBUT

Every flat fish from the flounder to the skate was called a *butt* in Old English. This held true for the largest of the flounders, *Hippoglossus hippoglossus,* which often weighed four hundred pounds and measured eight feet in length. So prized was *Hippoglossus* five centuries or so ago that what one naturalist called the "hallowed giant of all the demersal species" was eaten only on Church holy days and became known as the *haly* (holy) *butt.* No longer is the fish reserved for holy days, but it is still known as the *halibut* or "holy flounder." William Cowper actually wrote a poem in praise of halibut, or himself, concluding:

Thy lot thy brethren of the slimey fin
Would envy, could they know that thou wast doomed
To feed a bard and to be prais'd in verse.

Cowper has been criticized by the epicurean Saintsbury,
who found the "abominable Brobdingnagian dab" to be
"second-rate" eating, and by Ivor Brown, who writes:
"The notion of fish pining to become the raw material of
indifferent, or even of the best poetry and to serve as the
sustenance of human authorship is one which is beyond
comment."

HANGDOG LOOK

It's said that hunting dogs living in the great English country houses of the past, eating scraps tossed from the table,
and sleeping as close to the fire as they could get, were
kept orderly by special handlers who broke up dog fights,
whipped their charges, and even hanged incorrigible dogs.
Shakespeare, no dog lover, does refer to the hanging of
dogs five times in his plays. I've been unable to find
records of any actual case of a dog hanging at the time, but
as late as 1906 a dog accused of aiding a man in a robbery
was sentenced to death by a Swiss court (see E. R. Evans's
*The Criminal Prosecution and Capital Punishment of An-
imals,* 1906). Ten years later, in fact, an Erwin, Tennessee, mob lynched an *elephant* named Mary that had run
amok and killed a man, stringing her up with cable! During
the Middle Ages bulls, pigs, mules, roosters, rats, mice,
weevils, locusts, slugs, and many other animals were executed for one reason or another. Often they were dressed
in human clothing at their trials.

In any case, since the late seventeenth century anyone
with a cringing, abject appearance, or a base, sneaky de-

meanor has been said to have a *hangdog look*. Whether real or the product of someone's imagination, the allusion was originally to a despicable, degraded person fit only to hang a dog, or to be hanged like a dog. Nowadays a *hangdog look* has almost entirely lost its meaning of contemptible and sneaky and generally describes someone browbeaten, defeated, intimidated, or abject—someone who looks a little like a bloodhound.

HARRIDAN

In French *haridelle* means a worn-out old wreck of a horse. From this word comes the English *harridan*, a haggard, disreputable old woman, a vicious or violent old hag.

TO HAVE A LARK

The meadowlark used to be considered a game bird, and young people in the sixteenth and seventeenth centuries often hunted the bird for sport with nets, having a good time when they did so. This may have inspired the expression *to have a lark,* but the origin of the phrase is uncertain, and it could just as well have its roots in the English dialectal *lake*, "sport," which derives from the Anglo-Saxon word *lac*, "contest." At any rate, the expression was a common one by the nineteenth century.

HENPECKED, PECKING ORDER

The *pecking order* among hens, according to the famous
study made by biologist W. C. Allee, has a definite prestige
pattern: hens, like many humans, male and female, freely
peck at other hens below their rank and submit to pecking
from those above them. Although hens rarely peck at
roosters in the barnyard, where the rooster is the cock of
the walk, it was widely believed in the seventeenth century
that they often pulled feathers from young roosters below
them in the pecking order. This led to the comparison of
domineering wives to aggressive hens. Samuel Butler defined the term first; Dryden complained that he was hen-
pecked, and Steele called Socrates "the undoubted head of
the Sect of the Hen-pecked." There was even a noun, *hen-
peck,* for a wife who domineers over her husband. Byron,
in *Don Juan,* wrote the celebrated couplet:

> But—oh! ye lords of ladies intellectual,
> Inform us truly, have they not hen-peck'd you all.

HIDEBOUND

Cramped, constricted people, those who are rigidly opin-
ionated, have been called *hidebound* since the sixteenth
century. The word derives from a term applied to ema-
ciated cattle in days before veterinary science had made
many advances. Feeding and care of cattle was so poor in
England at the time that by winter the animals were often
thin and diseased and had lost the fatty tissue under the
skin. As a result their skin clung tightly to their bones, they
moved stiffly, and their hides couldn't be removed from

113

their backbones or ribs when they died. Their physical condition naturally suggested the inelastic, constipated minds of some people.

TO HIGHTAIL IT

Mustangs, rabbits, and other animals raise their tails high and flee quickly when they sense danger. Trappers in the American West noticed this over a century ago, probably when hunting wild deer, and invented the expression *to hightail* it, to make a fast getaway on foot, on a horse, or in a vehicle.

HIPPOPOTAMUS

Wrote the historian Macaulay, "I have seen the Hippo both asleep and awake, and I can assure you that asleep or awake, he is the ugliest of the Works of God." The *hippopotamus* was so named by the Greeks, who somehow thought it looked like a horse and, since it spent so much time in the water, called it "river horse," from the Greek *hippos,* "horse," and *potamos,* "river." It was also called the behemoth, monster, by the ancients. Hippos, which weigh up to 8,000 pounds, are in the water much of the time, sleeping and mating there, but they are good walkers and relatively fast runners, usually spending their nights out of the water. They are more closely related to the pig than to the horse. Bull hippos often fight to the death for females, but sometimes they have "defecation contests," in which they defecate and use their tails to catapult their feces about; the winner is the bull who excretes the most in the shortest time, or, to put it another way, euphemistically, throws the most *bull (q.v.)*.

114

HOBSON'S CHOICE

It is amazing how this expression has lasted for over three centuries, deriving as it does from the name of an obscure English carrier and innkeeper, Tobias or Thomas Hobson, who for some fifty years drove his stage from Cambridge to London sixty miles away, often at breakneck speeds, and kept some forty horses on the side to rent to students at Cambridge University. A humane man, who realized that "the scholars rid hard," he put his mounts on a strict rotation basis so that the best and most often chosen horses would not be ruined. When you rented a horse from Hobson, you rented the horse nearest the livery stable door, the one best rested, no matter what your preference or how many horses were available. In this way, Richard Steele wrote one hundred years after Hobson's death in an article in the *Spectator* (no. 509): "Every customer was alike well served according to his chance, and every horse ridden with the same justice." A *Hobson's choice* is therefore no choice at all, a take-it-or-leave-it proposition.

HOGAN'S GOAT

Goats do not eat tin cans (they eat the paper labels off them), but they do stink. For this reason, and no other, anything said to be like *Hogan's goat* (a play, a book, or whatever) is something that is very bad, that really stinks. Hogan is just a common name affixed to this Americanism that dates to the turn of the century—no real Hogan has anything to do with it. *Hogan's brickyard*, for a rough-hewn baseball diamond—one usually in a vacant lot—is a similar expression, but *Hogan*, a variety of cotton, is named for its nineteenth-century developer, William Hogan.

HOGWASH

"They in the kitchen, for jest, poured hogwash on her head," is the first mention of *hogwash* in English, according to the *OED*. This wasn't much of a joke, even in 1440, for hogwash was then the common term for the garbage or slops fed to pigs. Hogwash is thus not slang but colloquial English; even in its figurative sense of insincere talk, "garbage," or misleading propaganda, it dates back nearly three hundred years.

TO HOLD AT BAY

Surprisingly, scholars haven't been able to connect *to hold at bay* with hunting dogs that ran down big game like stags and held them at bay by barking or baying until the hunters arrived. Perhaps the baying of big-throated hounds bred for this purpose in medieval times did reinforce the expression, but *to hold at bay,* to hold at a standstill, to keep someone on the defensive, derives from the Old French phrase *tenir à bay,* which means to hold in a state of suspense, to hold in abeyance. The French expression, in turn, comes from the Italian *tenere a bada* meaning the same. *Bada* in the latter phrase indicates the state of suspense or expectation, deriving from the Latin *badare,* "to open the mouth." So although the idea of dogs baying at a trapped stag conveys the idea behind the expression perfectly, it really literally means to hold agape, or to hold with mouth open.

HOLD YOUR HORSES

Harness racing at American country fairs about a century and a half ago probably inspired the expression *hold your horses*. The amateur drivers, frequently young and inexperienced, often started their charges before a race had begun, leading the starter and the spectators to shout, "Hold your horses!" By the 1840s the expression was being used to urge human patience in general.

HORSE LATITUDES

The most interesting story about the meaning of these regions of calms, found at thirty degrees north and south latitudes, is that sailing ships carrying horses to America became becalmed and had to throw horses overboard to lighten the vessels and take advantage of any slight breeze that did blow up. It's also possible that the name is a translation of *golfo de las yeguas,* gulf of the mares, which was the Spanish name for the ocean between Spain and the Canary Islands and compares the fickleness of mares with the fickle winds in these latitudes. In contrast, the Spaniards called the ocean from the Canary Islands to the West Indies, which usually had smooth and favorable winds, the *golfo de las damas,* gulf of the ladies.

A HORSE OF A DIFFERENT COLOR

Cut into the chalk downs of Berkshire, England, is the enormous crude outline of a galloping white horse covering some two acres. The figure possibly dates back to Saxon times, when a white horse was the emblem of Saxons invading Britain, and over the ages local residents have kept it clear of overgrowth. It is thought that this might be the source of the expression *a horse of a different color,* something of a different nature from what is under consideration, for the White Horse of Berkshire changes from green to white periodically when the locals clear grass and weeds from its outline. The expression may, however, come from races in medieval tournaments, where armored knights were distinguished by the color of their horses. A favored knight might have lost a race, leading one of his supporters to say, "That's a horse of a different color," as the winner crossed the finish line. But both explanations are conjectures. The phrase is first alluded to in Shakespeare's *Twelfth Night,* Shakespeare using the expression as if it were quite familiar to his audience.

HORSELAUGH

A *horselaugh* is a loud, coarse, vulgar laugh, a guffaw. The word probably alludes to the loud neigh of a lusty horse, but an obscure pun on the word *horse* has also been suggested as a source. The expression has been common since Pope used it in 1710.

118

HORSEPOWER

Horsepower is actually about one and a half times the power of a horse. When seeking a way to indicate the power exerted by his steam engine, James Watt calculated that a strong dray horse averaged 22,000 foot-pounds per minute working at a gin on an eight-hour-a-day basis. Increasing this by 50 percent he got 33,000 foot-pounds, which has ever since been one horsepower: "The standard theoretical unit of rate of work, equal to the raising of 33,000 pounds one foot high in one minute."

HORSERADISH,
HORSE CHESTNUT

There is apparently no truth to old tales that the fiery *horseradish* (*Armoracia lapathifolia*) is so named because it was once used to cure horses of colds, or because it made a good seasoning for horse meat. *Horse* is used as an adjective before a number of plants to indicate a large, strong, or coarse kind. Others include the *horse cucumber, horsemint,* and *horse plum.* The horseradish is of course hotter, and has a much larger root and leaves, than the ordinary radish. However, many plants *are* named after the horse because they were used to feed or treat horses or because they resemble the animal. The *horsebean* is used as horse feed; *horse bane* was supposed to cause palsy in horses; the *horse-eye bean* was thought to resemble a horse's eye; and the pods of *horse vetch* are shaped like horseshoes. The *horse chestnut,* Gerard says in his famous *Herbal* (1597), bears its name because "people of the East countries do with the fruit thereof cure their horses of the cough . . . and such like diseases." But the horse chestnut nut is big, too, and when a slip is cut off the tree "obliquely close to a joint, it presents a miniature of a horse's hock and foot, shoe and nails." Incidentally, Samuel Pepys in his *Diary* mentions a *horseradish ale,* ale flavored with horseradish, which must have been hot indeed.

HOT DOG

Concessionaire Harry Stevens was the first to serve grilled frankfurters on a split roll—at the Polo Grounds, home of baseball's now defunct New York Giants, in about 1900. Frankfurters, so named because they had originally been made in Frankfurt, Germany, had been sold here long before this, but never with "the works"—heated roll, mustard, relish, et cetera. According to Stevens, they were dubbed *hot dogs* by that prolific word inventor, sports cartoonist T. A. Dorgan, when he sampled the franks on a roll. "Tad" possibly had in mind the fact that many people believed frankfurters were made from dog meat at the time, and no doubt heard Stevens's vendors crying out, "Get your red hots!" on cold days. Dorgan even drew the hot dog as a dachshund on a roll, leading the indignant Coney Island Chamber of Commerce to ban the use of the term *hot dog* by concessionaires there (they could only be called Coney Islands, red hots, and frankfurters).

TO HOUND SOMEONE

Hound derives from the common Teutonic *hund,* related to *hunt,* and may be related to the Teutonic verb *hinpan,* "to seize," in reference to big hunting dogs that actually

120

seized their prey. Eventually, however, the designation *hound* was reserved for hunting dogs that followed their quarry by scent. There were many varied breeds of these from early times, but all were noted for their tenacity as well as for their keen sense of smell. Hounds would follow a trail for hours, doubling back to find a scent if they lost it. By the late sixteenth century their grim persistence had suggested the expression *to hound someone,* to pursue someone relentlessly with the determination of a hound.

HOUYHNHNMS

These, of course, are the intelligent breed of horses that Jonathan Swift created in *Gulliver's Travels* (1726). Swift said he coined their name from the characteristic whinny of a horse as it sounded to him. The talking horses, endowed with reason, ruled over the brutish *Yahoos,* another word coined by Swift in the book. *Gulliver's Travels* also gives us *brobdingnagian,* for any immense thing, after the giants Gulliver encounters in the county of Brobdingnag, and *lilliputian,* after Lilliput, a country of tiny people. Knowing that *Houyhnhnms* is pronounced *whinims* makes it a little easier to recite Alexander Pope's poem "Mary Gulliver to Capt. Lemuel Gulliver" about the Houyhnhnms:

Nay would kind Jove my organ so dispose
To hymn harmonious Houyhnhnms through the nose
I'd call the Houyhnhnm, that high-sounding name;
Thy children's noses should all twang the same.

HUMBUG

This word for a fraud or hoax has long outlived those purists who so vehemently attacked it when it entered the language from underworld slang in the 1750s. No one knows just where *humbug* came from. Several authorities suggest the Irish *uim bog,* "soft copper," referring to debased money with which James II flooded England from the Dublin mint. Then there is the improbable guess that it derives from Hamburg, Germany, the center of German propaganda during the Franco-Prussian War. But *bug* in its slang sense had meant to cheat or "sting" before *humbug* was coined, and in former times people expressed approbation, perhaps even false encouragement, by humming. Then again, since the original meaning of bug is "bogey," a *humbug* may first have been a really harmless bug that hums and frightens us. Dickens's Scrooge with his "Bah, humbug!" gave the word great popularity worldwide, as did P. T. Barnum, "the Prince of Humbug," who often lectured on humbuggery and wrote that "the American people like to be humbugged."

HUSH PUPPY

These cakes of deep-fried cornmeal batter, very popular in the South, have only been traced back to the time of World War I; at least the name isn't recorded before then. The most common explanation for the odd name is that hunters tossed bits of the cakes to their dogs, telling them to *"hush, puppy."* A perhaps more authentic version notes that the cakes were first made in Florida, where people often fried fish outdoors in large pans, attracting dogs who

122

would whine and bark. To quiet the dogs, the cook would fry up some cornmeal cakes and throw them to the dogs, shouting, "Hush, puppies!"

HUSKY

Any man called *husky,* "stocky and muscular," is actually being compared to a sled dog—specifically, to a *husky,* or Eskimo dog, a strong breed capable of pulling great loads and covering sixty miles a day. Husky is used loosely for any arctic dog, but the breed is a recognized one. An unusual animal that yelps or howls like a wolf, although not closely related to the wolf, the husky normally feeds on fish and sleeps without shelter in the snow. Its name is a corruption of either the Tinneh Indian *uskimi,* an Eskimo; *Esky,* English slang for Eskimo; or the word *Eskimo* itself. Early explorers in the far North named the dog after the natives who bred it, and the dog's name was later applied to trappers who exhibited the breed's vigor, endurance, and stocky build.

Eskimo itself is an Algonquian word meaning "eaters of raw flesh." The Eskimos do not recognize it. They proudly call themselves *Innuit,* "the people," or "the human beings."

I SMELL A RAT

No one can say with irrefragable certainty how *I smell a rat* originated, but the allusion may be to a cat smelling a rat while being unable to see it. Terriers and other rat-hunting dogs could also be the source. The expression dates back to about 1780, but long before that *to smell* was used figuratively for to suspect or discern intuitively, as when Shakespeare wrote "Do you smell a fault?" in *King Lear.* St. Hilarion, the Syrian hermit who died about 371, could allegedly tell a person's vices or virtues simply by smelling his person or clothing.

IN THE BAG

It is usually assumed that this metaphor derives from hunting, where shot birds and other small game are trophies already safely in the game bag. *Bag* has been used as an abbreviation for game bag since at least the fifteenth century, but the expression *in the bag* is first recorded in 1925. William Bancroft Miller, writing in *Verbatim* (February 1977), offers another explanation, attributing the phrase to cockfighting: "Until comparatively recent years, it was common to transport game chickens to the scene of battle in cloth bags rather than in the comfortable and elaborate carrying cases now in vogue, and the roosters were not removed until the fight was about to begin. A cocker, confident of the prowess of his feathered warrior, would say that victory was *in the bag* for him." Neither theory is supported by quotations and neither explains the sinister implication these words often have, for the expression frequently means rigged or fixed, its offshoot *bagman* meaning a corrupt person who collects graft.

IN THE DOGHOUSE

Since *doghouse,* as a synonym for dog kennels, can be traced back to at least 1611, we'd expect that the expression *in the doghouse,* out of favor or undergoing punishment, would be of ancient origin. The phrase, however, seems to be an Americanism that is first recorded at the turn of the century. One guess is that the term originated during the African slave trade, when Yankee sailors locked the hatches at night to prevent slaves from escaping and slept on deck in tiny sleeping cubicles called "doghouses." But there are no quotations to support this theory and most authorities believe *in the doghouse* originally referred to wives punishing their husbands; that is, a domineering wife confining a "gay dog" who roved too much to his own home, or "doghouse," not letting him out nights.

JACKANAPES

Applied to any pretentious upstart who apes his betters, the word *jackanapes* probably comes from the nickname of William de la Pole, Duke of Suffolk. Jack was a common name for a tame male ape in England at the time (attached to the word, as it was to jackrabbit, jackass, and others), and Suffolk's coat of arms bore the clog and chain of a trained monkey. When, in 1450, the duke was arrested and beheaded at sea off Dover for alleged treason against Henry VI, he was derisively styled "the Ape-clogge" and later won the nickname Jack Napes or Jackanapes. The ending might mean "of Naples," the source of apes brought to England in the early fifteenth century, but there is little doubt that the word earned its popularity and present meaning through Suffolk's nickname, which was even recorded in a satirical song of the day. There have been other theories, such as one relating to the "Jack o' nails" face card in a fourteenth-century Saracen card game, but the weight of evidence falls on the unfortunate Duke of Suffolk as surely as the axe fell upon his neck. Suffolk, incidentally, may have been the victim of a frame-up by the Duke of York.

JENNY HANIVER

During idle hours at sea, sailors would sometimes shape and carve out strange mummies from dried skates or rays they had caught, manipulating these sea creatures so that they looked half human. Back in port gullible collectors often purchased these "mermaids," "dragons," and other fantastic creations, believing them to be real. This provided the seamen with an extra source of income and the incentive to continue their artistic endeavors. For three hundred years, beginning in the thirteenth century, sailors turned out such *Jenny Hanivers,* many specimens lasting for six hundred years and more, but no one can say for sure why they were so named. Perhaps the surname is a corruption of Antwerp, a bustling seaport of the time, but it is just as possible that some anonymous sailor bestowed the name of a real woman on the lifelike mummies. P. T. Barnum helped launch his career with a Jenny Haniver he claimed was a mermaid captured in the "Feejee" Islands, sending it on tour around the country. Actually, it was a monkey's torso sewed to the head of a fish. But then Barnum claimed that "there should be poetic license in mermaids."

JERSEY

Jersey, the largest of England's Channel Islands, was named for the Caesars, having been called *Caesarea* when the Romans ruled over it, *Jersey* being simply a corruption of *Caesarea.* In the eighth century B.C., *ey,* the suffix of the word *Jersey,* meant "an island," so therefore *Jersey* is "the island of Caesar," or "Caesar's island." Little evidence of the Roman occupation remains in Jersey or any of the islands in the English Channel. The Romans added the island to their empire after the Gauls had ruled there and, except for coins showing that their money circulated for over five hundred years, the only evidence of their occupation is traces of Roman buildings found in Alderney. Jersey also refers to a breed of cattle, raised on Jersey and noted for yielding milk with high butterfat content. (See also *Caesar.*)

JINX

Baseball Hall of Famer Christy Mathewson was among the first to use the word *jinx* in print when he wrote in his *Pitching in a Pinch* (1912): "A jinx is something which brings bad luck to a ballplayer." Big Six didn't know that the word may owe its life to a bird called the jynx whose name means "a charm or spell." The jynx, known in America as the wrynecked woodpecker or wryneck, takes its name from the Latin *iynx* for the bird. In the Middle Ages this *rara avis,* with its grotesque, twisted neck, its odd breeding and feeding habits, its harsh, strident cries during migration, and its near silence the rest of the time, was thought to have occult powers. Jynx feathers were used to make love philters and black magic charms, and the bird's name itself came to mean a charm or spell, especially a black magic spell, on a selected victim. It is easy to see how the slang term *jinx* arose from *jynx,* but the long flight of the jynx from medieval times to the printed page circa 1912 is not easily explained.

JUMBO

JUMBO THE ONLY MASTODON ON EARTH . . . THE GENTLE AND HISTORIC LORD OF BEASTS . . . THE TOWERING MONARCH OF HIS MIGHTY RACE . . . THE PRODIGIOUS PET OF BOTH ENGLAND AND AMERICA . . . STEADILY GROWING IN TREMENDOUS HEIGHT AND WEIGHT . . . JUMBO, THE UNIVERSAL SYNONYM FOR STUPENDOUS THINGS . . .

All in one handbill. Thus P. T. Barnum, in his subdued fashion, advertised an elephant whose name became "the universal synonym for stupendous things." Barnum purchased the fabled elephant from the London Zoological Society in 1881 for "The Barnum and Bailey Greatest Show on Earth." Jumbo, captured by a hunting party in 1869, was one of the largest elephants ever seen in West Africa; the natives called the six-and-a-half-ton beast by the Swahili word *jumbo,* meaning "chief." He became a great favorite in the London Zoo, giving rides to thousands of children, and his sale to the American showman caused quite an uproar. When Barnum's agent excitedly cabled that Jumbo was lying in a London street blocking traffic, Barnum replied, "Let him lie as long as he likes. Great advertisement." Within six weeks the incomparable P.T. had reaped $336,000 from his $30,000 investment, and he made Jumbo's name a synonym for "huge" throughout America and the world.

KANGAROO

A very old story that may well be true says that Captain James Cook and his shipmate, naturalist Sir Joseph Banks, spotted a kangaroo during their exploration of the South Pacific (1768–1771) and asked an Australian native the animal's name. The man answered, "I don't understand you," in his own tongue, and Cook thought that this expression, which sounded something like *kangaroo*, was the animal's name and adopted it as such. This story isn't told by Cook or Banks, but no better explanation has been found for *kangaroo*, which never appeared in any European tongue before the end of the eighteenth century and has not been traced to any Australian dialect. Cook believed that kangaroo was the name given to the animal by natives in Queensland, but at least three later explorers wrote that the name was unknown to any Australian natives before Europeans introduced it. These explorers reported that various names were used by different tribes for the animal—including *patagaran, patagorong,* and *moane*—none of them remotely resembling kangaroo (or *kangooroo,* as Cook first spelled it). The kangaroo, a marsupial that carries its young in a pouch and whose newborn offspring are the size of bumblebees, is found only in Australia, the only continent composed of one country and the only continent that has never had an internal war or revolution.

KANGAROO COURT

While *kangaroo court* may have originated in Australia, it was first recorded in America during the California gold rush. According to one story, the source for the term was kangaroos in Australia's backcounty, who when out of spear range sat staring dumbly at men for long periods of time before leaping off for the horizon, their staring similar to the dumb stares of jurors sitting on a mock jury and their leaping away suggesting the quick decisions of such an extralegal court. But there are no quotations supporting the use of kangaroo court in Australia at any time. The expression could have been coined in America, based on the several uses of the word *kangaroo* in England for anything unusual or eccentric. Another guess is that Americans familiar with the kangaroo's jumping habits, or Australian forty-niners with gold fever, invented *kangaroo court* as a humorous term for courts that tried "claim jumpers," miners who seized the mining claims of others.

KIBITZER

What does a little bird have to do with those givers of un-
solicited, unnecessary, uncalled-for advice whom we all en-
counter at one time or another? It appears that German
cardplayers of the sixteenth century found meddlesome
onlookers just as annoying as cardplayers do today. The
constant, gratuitous "advice" of these chatterers reminded them of the *Kiebitz*, the lapwing or plover, whose
shrill cries frightened game away from approaching hunters. Thus all *kibitzers* are named for this troublesome bird,
our pewit, which the Germans used to coin their word *kie-
bitzen*, "to look on at cards."

TO KICK THE BUCKET

A suicide who stands on a pail, slips a noose around his
neck, and kicks the pail or bucket out from under him
would be the logical choice for the origin of this old slang
term meaning "to die." But some etymologists say no, the
phrase comes from an entirely different source. Slaughtered hogs, their throats slit, used to be hung from their
heels, their feet tied to a wooden block. The rope would
then be thrown over a pulley, which hoisted the animals
up. Because hoisting the block was similar to raising a
bucket from a well, the wooden block came to be called a
"bucket," and the dying struggles of the hogs kicking
against this bucket gave birth to the phrase. There are
other theories, however, and this old expression—it may
date back to the sixteenth century—must be marked "of
uncertain origin."

TO KILL THE FATTED CALF

These words mean to prepare a warm welcome and are taken from the biblical parable of the prodigal son, Luke 15:11–24. When the prodigal son saw the error of his ways and came home from the "far country" where he had "wasted his substance with riotous living," his father commanded the servants: "Bring forth the best robe, and put it on him; and put a ring on his hand; and shoes on his feet: And bring hither the fatted calf, and kill it; and let us eat and be merry: For this my son was dead, and is alive again; he was lost, and is found. And they began to be merry."

KNEE-HIGH TO A GRASSHOPPER

Knee-high to a toad, recorded in 1814, was the original of this Americanism, and *knee-high to a mosquito* as well as *knee-high to a frog* appeared before it came on the scene some thirty-seven years later. But *knee-high to a grasshopper* has outlasted all the others, including the later *knee-high to a duck.* It is generally used in comparisons, emphasizing youth, smallness, or remoteness in time. There are some 120,000 varieties of grasshoppers, and to be literally knee-high or tibia-high to one a person would have to range from one millimeter tall to a little more than an inch tall.

The Utes were called the Grasshopper Indians because they used grasshoppers for food in dishes like *grasshopper pie.*

LAME DUCK

Before the adoption of the Twentieth Amendment to the Constitution in 1930 congressmen who were defeated for election in November elections still held office until the following March 4. These congressmen were called *lame ducks* because they were mostly ineffectual, although they could help pass legislation embarrassing to an incoming administration. The "Lame Duck Amendment" eliminated them, but lame duck appointments to diplomatic and other posts can still be made by a defeated, outgoing president. No one is sure where the term *lame duck* comes from. It originated about 125 years ago and may have been suggested by the British lame duck, a person who has lost all his money, who has been financially crippled on the stock exchange. On the other hand it could be native born, a qualification of the American phrase *a dead duck,* an out-going congressman being not quite dead yet, merely lamed until March 4 of the following year.

LAZY AS LUDLAM'S DOG

This old proverb refers to a dog belonging to a certain Mrs. Ludlam, an English sorceress, who lived in Surrey near Farnham. Her dog was so lazy that when strangers approached he always lay down or leaned up against a wall to bark, or didn't even bother to bark at all—there are several versions of the tale. A variation on the phrase is *as lazy as David Lawrence's dog,* or *as lazy as Lawrence's dog.*

TO LEAD BY THE NOSE

The allusion here is to animals like oxen, horses, and asses, which from early times were led around by bit and bridle or by a rope attached to a ring hanging from the septum of the nose. Even wild animals, such as bears and camels, were led around Roman arenas by a rope attached to a ring in the nose. Therefore, someone who leads another by the nose dominates him or holds him under submission. The idea is found in the Bible (Isaiah 37:29): "Because thy rage against me, and thy tumult, is come up into mine ears, therefore will I put my hook in thy nose, and my bridle in thy lips, and I will turn thee back by the way by which thou camest."

LEEUWENHOEK'S
LITTLE ANIMALS

These animal cubs had divers colors, some being whitish, others pellucid; others had green and very shining little scales, others again were green in the middle, and before and behind white, others greyish. And the motion of most of them in the water was so swift, and so various upwards, downwards and round about, that I confess I could not but wonder at it.

Anton von Leeuwenhoek (1632–1723), a former Dutch linen maker who designed a very powerful single lens microscope, changed the course of science with his observations of the "animalcules" in a drop of pond water. He often wrote descriptions like the one above, which he sent to the Royal Society of London on September 7, 1674, and his observations helped disprove the doctrine of spontaneous generation (that eels are generated from sand, grubs from wheat, and so on), making *Leeuwenhoek's little animals* a phrase that has lived for centuries.

A LEOPARD DOESN'T CHANGE
ITS SPOTS

Leopards are so named because they were once thought not to be a separate species but a cross between the lion (*leo*) and the *pard,* a Tibetan wildcat or panther. Like the creature's name, the saying *a leopard doesn't change its spots* goes back to ancient times. It is an allusion to the pessimistic rhetorical question found in Jeremiah 13:23: "Can the Ethiopian change his skin, or the leopard his spots? then may also do good you that are accustomed to do evil." The *leopon* is the cross of a lion and a leopard; one such animal at the London Zoo had the jaw of a lioness and the spots of a leopard.

LET SLEEPING DOGS LIE

Chaucer seems to have expressed the idea first in *Troilus and Criseyde* (1374), though he put it in the reverse form: "It is nought good a slepyng hound to wake." For at least four hundred years the saying remained basically the same, until in the nineteenth century it became the familiar *let sleeping dogs lie,* leave well enough alone.

LET THE CAT OUT OF THE BAG

Rural people aren't usually country bumpkins. In days past city slickers had to beware of buying a farmer's pig in a poke, a pig brought to market in a bag, because the "pigs" inside such pokes were sometimes cats the canny country folk had substituted for suckling pigs. A merchant who bought a pig in a poke was stuck with it, but one who wisely opened the poke often *let the cat out of the bag,* revealing the crafty farmer's secret. The deceptive practice was widespread enough in England for both expressions to be common well over four centuries ago. It may also have led to the expression *left holding the bag,* because anyone falling for the farmer's ploy would be left with an empty bag on opening it, the cat inside darting away. This is only a guess, however; the empty bag could just as easily have been an empty purse held by a man robbed by his servant, and there are a dozen similar possibilities.

LET'S TALK TURKEY

An old story, frequently embellished and reprinted over the years, has it that back in colonial days a white hunter unevenly divided the spoils of a day's hunt with his Indian companion. Of the four crows and four wild turkeys they had bagged, the hunter handed a crow to the Indian, took a turkey for himself, then handed a second crow to the Indian and put still another turkey in his own bag. All the while he kept saying, "You may take this crow and I will take this turkey," or something similar, but the Indian wasn't as gullible as he thought. When he had finished dividing the kill, the "ignorant savage" protested: "You talk all turkey for you. You never once talk turkey for me! Now I talk turkey to you." He then proceeded to take his fair share. Most scholars agree that from this probably apocryphal tale, first printed in 1830, comes the expression *let's talk turkey*, let's get down to real business.

TO LICK INTO SHAPE

Beres ben brought forthe al fowle and transformyd and after that my lychynge of the fader and moder they ben brought in to theyr kyndely shap.
—*The Pylgremage of the Sowle*, 1400

For at least ten centuries people believed that bear cubs were born just formless masses of grotesque flesh and that both Mama and Poppa Bear took turns literally licking them into shape. No one debunked this legend for so long because bears usually keep their cubs concealed a month or so after their birth and debunkers rarely ventured into bear dens for evidence. So the story was widely believed—by Pliny, Montaigne, and Shakespeare, among others—until and even after the discovery of America. By the time the marvelous tale was disproved the expression *to lick into shape,* to make ready, to make presentable, had a permanent place in the language.

TO LIONIZE

To lionize a person can be to show him sights worthy of him, the term taking its name from the old practice of showing visiting dignitaries the lions that used to be kept at the Tower of London menagerie, a major tourist attraction until it was abolished at the beginning of the nineteenth century. An earlier use of the word, however, is to lionize a person by making a fuss over him, by making him feel like a lion. Both expressions date back to the early 1800s.

A LION'S SHARE

In Aesop's fable about the lion who hunted with several other animals, the spoils of the hunt were demanded by the lion. He claimed one-quarter share as king of the beasts; a second because he was braver than any other animal; a third for his mate and cubs; "and as for the fourth, let he who will dispute it with me." In another version of the tale the lion says the last share belongs to everyone, "But touch it if you dare!" In any case from "The Lion and His Fellow-Hunters" derives our term *a lion's share,* all or nearly all of anything, and *leonine contract,* a completely one-sided agreement.

A LITTLE BIRD TOLD ME

One scholar suggests that the old familiar saying may have originated with the similar-sounding Dutch expression *Er lif t'el baerd,* which means "I should betray another." More likely the idea behind the phrase is in the noiseless flight of a bird, reinforced by a biblical passage from Ecclesiastes 10:20: "Curse not the king, no not in thy thought . . . for a bird of the air shall carry the voice, and that which hath wings shall tell the matter." Used by Shakespeare and Swift, the expression dates back to at least the sixteenth century.

LIVING HIGH OFF THE HOG

Because the best cuts of meat on a hog—the hams, pork chops, bacon, tenderloin, and spare ribs—are high up on a hog's sides, American southerners used the expression *eating high on the hog* for good eating, as opposed to *eating low on the hog*—eating the pig's feet, knuckles, jowls, and sow belly, today well known as "soul food." By extension *living high off the hog* came to mean living prosperously.

LOADED FOR BEAR

Any pioneer hunter who went out into the woods made sure that his gun carried a charge powerful enough to bring down a bear, for the most dangerous of American animals ranged everywhere. *Loaded for b'ar* eventually came to mean not only to be prepared for bear, but to be well prepared for any contingency, and toward the end of the nineteenth century it became a typical American term meaning "drunk," though this last is rarely heard anymore.

LOBSTER

Strangely enough, our thrifty Puritan ancestors actually threw the redoubtable lobster away, or used him for fertilizer or bait. Perhaps this was because he so much resembled an insect, which New England lobstermen still call *Homarus americanus* to this day. The lobster is, in fact, a kind of "bug," the word *lobster* itself being a melding of two foreign words: the Latin *locusta* meaning "locust," and the Anglo-Saxon *loppe,* which means "spider." Like all shellfish and insects, lobsters are really invertebrate arthropods, and neither the entomological nor the etymological comparisons helped early American appetites any. Today lobster is fast replacing steak as America's favorite restaurant food, though it may yet price itself out of the competition.

There is some confusion on menus as to what is true lobster. Real lobster is not the "freshwater lobster" that the French call *écrevisse,* or crawfish, a small European crustacean with no claws; or the warm-water spiny lobster from which lobster tails are obtained, which is labeled *langosta* or *langouste* in some restaurants; or even "the Shlobster," nature's newest seafood public relations product, which is in reality a giant shrimp. True lobsters include only *Homarus americanus,* often called Maine or North Atlantic lobsters; the smaller blue lobster of Europe, *Homarus vulgaris;* and *Nephrops norvegicus,* the orange Norwegian lobster, variously called "lady lobster,"

141

"scampi," "prawn," or "crevette rose." It is these "great and fat and luscious creatures," as an early writer called them, that have inspired all the memorable references in literature to the kingly crustacean, from Rabelais's advice that lobster be cooked "red as a cardinal's hat" to John Dos Passos's confession that "James Stephens, along with broiled live lobster, is one of the reasons I will never commit suicide." As for Art Buchwald's apocryphal Society for the Prevention of Cruelty to Lobsters, the very real Massachusetts Society for the Prevention of Cruelty to Animals suggests that a lobster be "anesthetized" (so that he can be boiled without "visible signs of discomfort") by first soaking him in a mixture of two quarts of cold water and one pound of salt.

During the Revolutionary War Americans called British soldiers *lobsters* and *lobsterbacks* as well as *redcoats* because of their red jackets.

LOBSTER NEWBURG

According to old Delmonico menus, the name should be *lobster Wenberg,* not *lobster Newburg.* Actually, this delectable lobster dish should have blazoned the name of Benjamin J. Wenberg (1835–1885), a late-nineteenth-century shipping magnate, across the pages of menus everywhere. But gastronomical tradition has it that he was foolish enough to displease the great restaurateur Lorenzo Delmonico. Wenberg had discovered the dish in South America and on his return described it glowingly to Delmonico's owner. Lorenzo soon instructed his chef to prepare the shelled lobster in its rich sauce of sherry, thick cream, and egg yolks, serving the dish to his wealthy patron and naming it *Lobster Wenberg* in his honor. So it remained on Delmonico's menu for almost a month, until

Wenberg, well in his cups, got into a fight in the estimable restaurant's main dining room and was bodily ejected. The next day the dish appeared on an enraged Lorenzo's menu as *Lobster Newburg,* perhaps in honor of the city on the Hudson, which name it retains today.

TO LOCK HORNS

Possibly New Englanders who witnessed moose fiercely battling over a female, their massive horns locked together, invented our expression for a violent clash. There is no evidence of this in the first American literary use of the phrase in 1839, however. When Swinburne used the phrase in 1865, he spoke of a heifer and her mate locking horns, which could also be the source of the expression. Moose have the largest antlers of any deer. It is said that their horns sometimes become so securely locked that the moose can't get free from one another and starve to death.

TO LOCK THE BARN DOOR
AFTER THE HORSE IS STOLEN

The venerable rustic aphorism for taking a precaution too late hangs in there; it is still heard in cities that haven't seen a barn for half a century. Back in England in the 1300s we would have recognized the expression, its first literary use being in John Gower's *Confessio Amantis* (1390): "For when the grete Stiede is stole, thanne he taketh hiede, and maketh the stable dore fast."

LOLLIPOP

Is the *lollipop* named after a racehorse? The story is that in the early 1900s one George Smith, a Connecticut candy manufacturer, "put together the candy and the stick" and named it in honor of Lolly Pop, the era's most famous racehorse, the name "lollipop" then becoming an exclusive trade name used by the Bradley-Smith company of New Haven. It is true that candy on a stick wasn't known in America before about 1908 and neither was the word *lollipop*. Smith may have invented the confection (there are no other claimants), and he may even have named his candy on a stick after the horse in question. But the word *lollipop* for a piece of sucking candy that dissolves easily in the mouth (*not* one, however, that is attached to a stick) was widely used in England as early as the late eighteenth century. It apparently derives from the English dialect word *lolly*, used in northern England to mean tongue, plus the word *pop*, in reference to the sound children make when sucking candy. Somehow lollipop remained unknown to Americans until the candy on a stick was invented in the early twentieth century, but this is not to say that the racehorse Lolly Pop couldn't have been named for the British word for sucking candy.

LONG IN THE TOOTH

Horses, whose gums recede as they grow older, showing more of their teeth, suggested this phrase for "aged," which probably dates back to the early 1800s. The saying has nothing to do with the teeth growing longer with age, although such is the case with some animals. Rats, for example, are doomed by nature to be voracious eaters because their teeth grow so long that they can actually pierce the roof of their mouth and enter their brain if they don't constantly gnaw and file them down.

LOVE ME, LOVE MY DOG

What the phrase means is "if you want to love me, you'll have to take me faults and all." Almost nine hundred years ago St. Bernard (1091–1153), famous abbot of the monastery of Clairvaux, said this in Latin: *Qui me amat, amat et canem meum.* Despite the canine association, he is not St. Bernard de Menthon (923–1008), who founded the Alpine shelter now called the Hospice of Great St. Bernard and after whom the *St. Bernard* dog (*q.v.*) is named.

LYNX-EYED

The wildcat (*Lynx rufus*) we now call a lynx doesn't have remarkable eyesight and isn't responsible for this expression. Most likely *lynx-eyed* meaning keen-sighted is a corruption of *Lyncus-eyed.* Lyncus, one of the Argonauts of Greek legend who sailed in search of the Golden Fleece, could make out objects up to nine miles distant and even see right through the earth. His name is related to the Greek *leussien,* "to see." The legendary half-panther and half-dog famed for its keen eyesight and called a lynx probably takes its name from Lyncus, and this creature may in turn be the namesake for the actual wildcat. A fierce fighter that goes for its adversaries' eyes when it attacks, the lynx or bobcat is also responsible for the expression *fight like a wildcat*. New York's Catskill Mountains are named after the wildcat, taking their name from the Dutch *Kaatskill*, or "wildcat creek," which Henry Hudson bestowed upon them and the river that is called the Hudson today.

MAD AS A HATTER

Lewis Carroll popularized but didn't invent this phrase with his creation of the Mad Hatter in *Alice's Adventures in Wonderland* (1865). *Mad as a hatter,* crazy, completely demented, was used by Thackeray in *Pendennis* (1850) and by that prolific Canadian phrase maker Thomas Haliburton in *The Clockmaker* (1837) almost thirty years before Carroll. Several explanations for the expression have been advanced. One holds that the phrase was originally *mad as an adder,* an adder being a venomous viper whose bite was once thought to cause insanity— British mispronunciation is supposed to have corrupted *adder* to *atter* and then to *hatter.* Australian miners, called *hatters,* and a bit mad because they worked alone so often, are another, slim, possibility. The curious metaphor is best explained by hatmaking itself, though. The mercuric nitrate long used in making felt hats often poisoned hatters, the poisoning effects of this mercurial compound causing men who worked with it for years to be afflicted with uncontrollable twitching muscles, a lurching gait, incoherent speech, and a confused mind. It is said that degrees of insanity were common in the hat trade, and there are a number of references in literature to mad or eccentric hatters; Sir John Tenniel's drawing of the Mad Hatter in *Alice* is a good clinical representation of them.

MAD AS A MARCH HARE

Erasmus used the words *mad as a marsh hare,* claiming that "hares are wilder in the marshes from the absence of hedges and cover." But Chaucer had the phrase *mad as a hare* before him, and *march hare* seems to have preceded *marsh hare* in use. Buck hares are wild frolickers in March, their breeding season, which has made them a synonym for lunacy for centuries. Lewis Carroll gave the expression new life with his creation of the March Hare in *Alice's Adventures in Wonderland.*

MAD AS A WET HEN

Hens don't become very upset from getting wet, so this old expression isn't a particularly accurate one. An Americanism that dates back to the early nineteenth century, it was apparently based on the false assumption that a hen, being exclusively a land animal, unlike, say, the duck, would go berserk if caught in the rain or douse with water. Better was the old expression *wet hen* for a prostitute.

TO MAKE A MOUNTAIN
OUT OF A MOLEHILL

In his "Ode to a Fly" the Greek satirist Lucian conveyed this same idea, to give something much greater importance than it deserves. His *to make an elephant out of a fly* remains a French and German phrase to this day, but for some unknown reason the expression never passed directly into English. Instead, the elephant became a mountain and the fly a molehill. Foxe's *Book of Martyrs* (1563) first recorded "makeying mountaines of Molehils."

TO MAKE FUR FLY

The cruel "sport" of trapping raccoons and setting dogs on them to see how long the coons could last may have suggested this expression to American pioneers. Certainly the air was filled with fur during such fights. By at least 1825 the saying meant to attack violently. In the autobiographical *A Narrative of the Life of David Crockett, of the State of Tennessee* (1834) we read: "I knew very well that I was in the devil of a hobble, for my father had been taking a few horns, and was in a good condition to make the fur fly."

TO MAKE ONE'S GORGE RISE

Hunting falcons are fierce creatures that store the food they eat in a pouch called the crop, or gorge. Their trainers in medieval times noticed that they frequently overate and vomited part of their food, which came to be called *gorge* after the pouch it came from. *To make one's gorge rise* therefore became a synonym for to make someone sick. The saying at first indicated extreme disgust and later expressed violent resentment against the persons who disgusted one, so that today the words mean to make a person violently angry.

TO MAKE ONE'S HAIR
STAND ON END

Surprisingly this metaphor isn't recorded before 1530, in a French phrase, but the idea behind it is found in the Bible (Job 4:14–15): "Fear came upon me, and trembling . . . the hair of my flesh stood up." The hair on cats, humans, and other animals can stand on end and become rigid with fear, or try to—the little muscles controlling this reaction work so well that even bald-headed men feel a prickling of the scalp from sudden terror. An English clergyman at an execution in the early nineteenth century observed the following: "When the executioner put the cords on the criminal's wrists, his hair, though long and lanky . . . rose gradually and stood perfectly upright, and so remained for some time, and then fell gradually down again." (See also *Goose Pimples.*)

MAN BITES DOG

"If a dog bites a man," editors used to instruct cub reporters, "that's an ordinary occurrence. But when a man bites a dog, that's *news."* The advice and the saying *man bites dog* can be traced back to Oliver Goldsmith's poem "Elegy on the Death of a Mad Dog," about a dog that "went mad and bit a man," which concludes with the lines:

> The man recover'd of the bite,
> The dog it was that died.

According to Partridge, this touching poem passed into folklore in a number of versions, possibly including a funny one where a man *did* bite a dog, and finally became the journalistic advice.

MAVERICK

Texas lawyer Samuel Augustus Maverick (1803–1870) reluctantly became a rancher in 1845 when he acquired a herd of cattle in payment for a debt. Maverick, a hero who was imprisoned twice in the war for independence from Mexico and was a signer of the Texas Declaration of Independence, eventually moved his cattle to the Conquistar Ranch on the Matagorda Peninsula fifty miles from San Antonio. But he was too involved in other activities to prove much of a rancher. When in 1855 he sold out to A. Toutant de Beauregard, their contract included all the unbranded cattle on the ranch. Since careless hired hands had failed to brand many of Maverick's calves, Beauregard's cowboys claimed every unbranded animal they came upon as a *maverick*. Sam Maverick never owned another cow, but his name soon meant any unbranded stock and later referred to any person who holds himself apart from the herd, a nonconformist.

MOLLY

Of the many tropical fish kept in millions of home aquariums only guppies are more popular than *mollies,* but few enthusiasts know that the fish takes its feminine name from a man. Count François Nicolas Mollien (1758–1850) wasn't a tropical fish collector—the hobby only dates back to about 1860—but a French financial genius who served several governments. Mollien was often consulted by Napoleon, who unfortunately refused to accept his advice against instituting his ill-fated "continental system." The tropical freshwater fish genus *Mollienisia* was irregularly named in Mollien's honor and since then all mollies with their female nickname bear this man's abbreviated surname. (See also *Guppy.*)

MONKEY WRENCH

One would think that the *monkey wrench* is so named because it's "monkeywise" or because the wrench's sliding jaws reminded someone of a monkey's chewing apparatus. This may be the case, but there is some reason to believe that the tool was named after its inventor. One source suggests that this mechanical wizard was London blacksmith Charles Moncke, but this theory is suspect since the British do not commonly call the tool a monkey wrench, using the terms *adjustable spanner wrench* or *spanner.* A more likely explanation turned up some years ago in a collection of undated clippings on word origins collected by a Boston doctor. One article from the Boston *Transcript,* appearing in the winter of 1932–1933, attributed the wrench's invention to a Yankee mechanic by the name of Monk employed by Bemis & Call of Springfield, Massachusetts. Monk supposedly invented the movable jaw for a wrench in 1856, and although it was given a special name at first, workers in his shop were soon calling it *Monk's wrench*. The tale has not been confirmed, but the 1856 date coincides with the first use of the word in the *Oxford English Dictionary* (1858), making the theory plausible. None of the big dictionaries makes an attempt to trace the word's origin, not even to say that the wrench resembles a monkey's jaw, just as a crane resembles a crane's neck.

As for the word *monkey,* it may derive from a proper name, too. In one Low German version of the Reynard the Fox animal tale, published in about 1480, *Moneke* is the son of Martin the Ape. Moneke probably took his name from the German surname Moneke, which has many variants, or from the Italian *monna,* "a female ape." Another possibility is the Italian *monicchia,* a nickname for a loquacious aged woman, whom the chattering, shriveled animal may have been thought to resemble. It is certain that the name for monkey persisted through the popularity of Reynard the Fox and the little moneke that the tale included.

MORE THAN ONE WAY
TO SKIN A CAT

"There are more ways of killing a cat than choking it with cream," was the older form of this British expression. This implied that a method of doing something was rather foolish, since cats like cream and wouldn't likely choke to death on it. But the saying changed in wording until it took on its present meaning—that there are more ways than one of accomplishing something. The expression shouldn't be confused with the American saying *skinning the cat,* which describes a child hanging from a tree branch, drawing his legs up through his arms and over the branch, and pulling himself into a sitting position atop it.

MYRMIDONS OF THE LAW

When the inhabitants of the island of Aegina were wiped out by a plague, the Greek god Zeus rewarded his son Aeacus, the island's leader, by creating new human beings from ants to repeople the place. According to Greek legend, these people were called *Myrmidons* after the tribe of ants (*myrmax*). The Myrmidons later followed Achilles to the Trojan War, in which they were noted for their faithful obedience and brutality. Their name is applied to officers of the law—policemen, sheriffs, and others—who carry out any order unthinkingly and without scruples.

N

N was originally a wavy line (〰) in Egyptian hieroglyphs and meant the sea or a fish. In Phoenician it was called *nun,* "a fish."

NAMES FOR YOUNG ANIMALS

Animals (generally)—younglet, youngling, offspring
Antelope—calf
Bear—cub
Beasts of prey—whelp
Beaver—kit
Birds—fledgling, nestling
Cat—pussy, kit, kitten, catling

Codfish—codling, sprat
Cow—calf
Deer—fawn, yearling
Dog—pup, puppy, whelp
Duck—duckling
Eagle—eaglet
Eel—elver
Elephant—calf
Fish (generally)—fry
Fowl—chick, chicken
Fowl (wild)—flapper
Fox—cub, pup
Frog—polliwog, tadpole
Goat—kid
Goose—gosling, grouse, cheeper
Grouse—cheeper
Hawk—eyas
Hen—pullet
Hippopotamus—calf
Horse—foal, yearling, colt (male),
    filly (female)
Kangaroo—joey
Lion—cub
Mackerel—blinker, tinker, spike
Owl—owlet
Partridge—cheeper
Pig—piglet, shoat, farrow, suckling
Pigeon—squab, squeaker
Quail—cheeper
Rabbit—bunny, kit
Rat—pup
Rhino—calf
Rooster—cockerel
Salmon—parr, smolt, grilse
Seal—pup
Shark—cub

Sheep—lamb, lambkin, cosset, hog
Swan—cygnet
Tiger—whelp, cub
Turkey—poult
Whale—calf
Zebra—foal

NEITHER HIDE NOR HAIR

In hide and hair, meaning "completely, wholly, every part," goes back to Chaucerian times, but its opposite, *neither hide nor hair,* is a nineteenth-century Americanism, probably arising on the frontier. A hungry predator devouring his prey "hide and hair" has been suggested as the source of the first metaphor, but that is hard to swallow for man or beast. Anyway, the reverse phrase means "nothing whatsoever," and its earliest record is in a book by Timothy Titcomb, the pseudonym of the American writer Josiah G. Holland, who founded *Scribner's Monthly:* "I haven't seen hide nor hair of the piece ever since."

NIGHTMARE, INCUBUS

Bad dreams in Roman times were attributed to demons called the *incubus* and *succubus.* The incubus (from the Latin *incubare,* "to lie on," which also gives us the word *incubate*) was said to consort with women in their sleep. This explained the heaviness or suffocation a woman might feel during a bad dream. The superstition was so widely believed in the Middle Ages that any woman who gave birth to a "witch" was supposed to have been visited by a male demon. The female counterpart of the *incubus* was

157

the *succubus* (from the Latin *suc* or *sub*, "under," and *cubare*, "to lie"), who slid beneath a male sleeper and gave him a terrible ride. There were laws against these demons in the Dark Ages, and their existence was recognized by the Church and state. Soon they became known as the *night hag, the riding of the witches,* and the *nightmare* as well. The nightmare, however, had nothing to do with a female horse, taking its name from *night,* plus the Anglo-Saxon *mare,* meaning "incubus." Nightmare eventually replaced the older Latin word *incubus,* which is now used to describe an oppressive load. Although the word wasn't born from a horse, it caught the popular imagination because of the graphic picture it suggested of a terrible horse bearing sleepers off on a frightening ride. (See also *Daymare.*)

NO ROOM TO
SWING A CAT

Though it doesn't originate with someone holding a cat by the tail and swinging it around his head, this phrase must have something to do with the old "sport" of swinging cats by the tails as targets for archers. The expression goes back to at least the mid-1600s, and "cat-o'-nine-tails" (*q.v.*) isn't recorded until about 1670, which makes it unlikely that the phrase originated with some sea captain having no room to punish a rebellious sailor with a "cat." The only other plausible explanation is that *cat* in this case refers to a sailor's hammock or *cot,* there being little room on olden ships to swing one, but there are no quotations to support this theory. (See also *To Fight like Kilkenny Cats.*)

NOT TO TURN A HAIR

This phrase means not to show any signs of distress, to be unruffled, unaffected by exertion or any agitation. This is a term from the stables, where the first sign of distress in a horse is sweating, which roughens the animal's coat, his hair remaining smooth and glossy as long as he keeps cool. Jane Austen first recorded the expression in *Northanger Abbey* (1818), writing of a horse: "He had not turned a hair till we came to Walcot church."

NOT WORTH A PLUG NICKEL

Since colonial times *an old plug,* or simply a *plug,* has meant an inferior horse, one with defects. From this expression came the term *plug* for a counterfeit coin, that is, a coin with defects, and the still common saying *not worth a plug nickel. Nickel* itself fits nicely in the phrase from an etymological point of view. Once the chief constituent of the United States five-cent piece, the metal nickel was christened by German miners who often found it when mining for the more expensive copper. In their disappointment they named nickel after a goblin called Nicholas that they blamed for such small mishaps. With the demise of the five-cent cigar, phone call, subway ride, and so on, *not worth a plug nickel* became more meaningful than ever.

O'DONOHUE'S WHITE HORSES

The fabled Irish chieftain O'Donohue is said to return to the Lakes of Killarney every seventh year on May Day riding his great white horse, gliding over the waters to sweet but unearthly music, a host of fairies preceding him and strewing his path with spring flowers. Waves created with foam on a windy day are thus known as *O'Donohue's white horses.* According to legend, at least one young and beautiful girl believed in O'Donohue so strongly that she threw herself in the water so that he would carry her off for his bride.

The term *white horses* is also used for crested waves, as in Matthew Arnold's poem "The Forsaken Merman":

> The wild horses play
> Champ and chafe and toss in the spray.

OLD BAT, ON A BAT

To call a woman an *old bat* is not to call her an old battle-ax, as many people believe. *Bat* is not a shortening of battle-ax here, but English slang for a prostitute that goes back to at least 1612. A bat was a prostitute who walked the streets; like a bat she usually worked at night, or, if she worked during the day, she hid out in dark recesses like a bat.

To go *on a bat,* a binge or a drinking spree, is similarly connected with the nocturnal bat—the "night bird," not the prostitute. Someone who goes on a bat often stays out all night. The first such bat recorded in literature, in 1848, describes the spree as taking place at night.

The winged, rodentlike bat was called by the colorful name *flittermouse* in days past. It figures in many expressions. (See also *Bats in Your Belfry; Like a Bat Out of Hell.*)

OLD STAMPING GROUNDS

An interesting theory connects this Americanism, used before the Revolution, with the mating of male prairie chickens, who congregated in spring on hills and performed elaborate courtship dances, stamping the hills bare. Another guess is that the stamping of stallions while they covered mares suggested the phrase. All that is known is that *stamping grounds* first referred to places where horses or other animals customarily gathered. It wasn't too long (1836) before the term described a place where people customarily gathered. The British definition of a stamping ground as "a place for amorous dalliance," like a lover's lane, gives some support to the prairie chicken and stallion theories. The expression is generally used by or about males.

ONE SWALLOW DOES NOT A SUMMER MAKE

The proverb was first recorded in English as "It is not one swallowe that bryngeth in somer. It is not one good qualitie that maketh a man good" (1539). However, Aristotle gave the Greek proverb "One swallow does not make a spring" long before in his *Nicomachaean Ethics.* The migratory swallow is still regarded as a harbinger of summer. The nests of some species, formed from the spawn of fish and seaweed bound together by the bird's solidified saliva, are used for bird's nest soup, among the most *recherché* of exotic foods. They are the subject of many legends—for instance, that they breed while in flight and that they bring good luck to any house they build a nest upon. Scandinavian tradition says that swallows hovered over the cross of Christ crying *Svala! svala* (Console! console!), hence their name *svalow,* "the bird of consolation." *One swallow does not a summer make* means that all one's troubles aren't over just because one difficulty is surmounted.

THE OO

Also called *Bishop's oo* (*Moho bishopi*) this most unusually named bird is a member of the honey eater family, birds that eat nectar and flowers as a part of their diet. The

Bishop of the bird's name honors American Charles Reed Bishop (1822–1915), who married a Hawaiian princess and became powerful in the islands' business and political affairs. *Oo* is simply the Hawaiian word for unknown, perhaps because so little was known about the bird before it was named.

OSTRACISM

Oysters were a staple of the early Greek diet, and where there are many oysters there must be many oyster shells. This situation led to the coining of the word *ostracism,* which comes directly from *ostrakon,* the Greek word for oyster shell. Ordinarily, voting in Athens was done by a show of hands. A vote of banishment, however, had to be written, as did any vote as serious as sending a person into exile for crimes against the democratic state. Because of the scarcity of paper or papyrus, the banishment ballot was usually written on common broken pieces of tile called *ostraka,* this name having first been applied to the shell of the oyster, which the tile somewhat resembled. The Athenians then bestowed the name *ostrakismos* upon the act of banishment itself, which gave us our word for to banish socially—to *ostracize.*

OSTRICHISM

Whole nations, fooled by falsehood, fear, or pride,
Their ostrich-heads in self-illusion hide.

So Thomas Moore wrote in his *Sceptic* (1808). The ostrich had a reputation for hiding its head in the sand as far back as 1623, when the expression is first recorded: "Like the Austridge, who hiding her little head, supposeth her great body obscured." The truth is that the flightless ostrich doesn't hide its head in the sand, though it does try to evade danger by lying flat on the ground with its long neck stretched out to create an imperceptible profile. The technique must work, for the ostrich is a long-lived bird, often living until fifty. At eight feet tall and 300 pounds, with eyes as big as tennis balls, the ostrich is the world's biggest living bird, but it can still run up to thirty miles an hour. Ostriches have also been said to swallow iron and diamonds (Shakespeare tells this old tale and it is true—fifty-three diamonds were found in the gizzard of one), hatch its young just by gazing at its eggs (which it doesn't, though its eggs at three pounds each are the world's largest), and disregard its young (actually, both male and female are good parents).

Brewer notes that "ostrich eggs are suspended in Eastern churches as symbols of God's watchful care because ostriches are thought to hatch eggs by gazing on them." Robert Southey has a poem ("Thalaba") noting this practice:

> Oh! even with such a look as fables say
> The mother ostrich fixes on her eggs,
> Till that intense affection
> Kindle its light of life.

The ostrich has given its name to the words *ostrich stomach,* a stomach that can digest anything, and *ostrichism,* "the policy of hiding the head like an ostrich," coined at the beginning of the nineteenth century. Obviously, the ostrich hiding its head in the sand is a useful metaphor, even if it is untrue. Vilhjalmur Stefansson had this to say about it in *Adventures in Error* (1936):

Consider what trouble we would get into if we did not have the literary ostrich and wanted to convey picturesquely the idea of that sort of wilful blindness from which we ourselves never suffer but which curiously afflicts our opponents. In pursuit of suitable analogy we might vainly canvass the whole animal kingdom. The ostrich-by-definition is, therefore, not only less trouble to deal with than a real bird; he is actually more useful and instructive than any real bird or beast. When we consider how often he has been used in sermon and precept we must admit that this model creature has contributed substantially not only to the entertainment and instruction of nature but also to the morality and grand goodness of the world.

PARTRIDGE, PARTRIDGE,
ALWAYS PARTRIDGE

Trace the roots of the word *partridge* back to the Greek *perdika,* "a partridge," and you'll find one of the oddest and most expurgated of bird name derivations. For the source for *perdika* is probably *perdesthai,* "to fart," the Greeks most likely naming the game bird for the sound the whirring wings of the rising bird made, which they thought resembled the breaking of wind.

A Greek legend says that Talus, the nephew of Daedalus, was killed by his uncle, who threw him into the sea while they argued about who invented the saw, possibly because Talus had been sleeping with Daedalus' mother. Talus flew off in the form of a partridge and became known as Perdix. Daedalus, condemned for the murder, fled from Athens to Crete, where he was eventually trapped by King

166

Minos. In order to escape he fashioned bird wings for himself and his son, Icarus, but Icarus flew too close to the sun, the wax on his wings melted, and he fell into the sea and drowned. While the gods had changed Talus into a partridge, Daedalus couldn't make his son into a bird.

Partridge, always partridge (*perdix, toujours perdix*) means too much of the same thing. It's said that the confessor of a French king admonished him for infidelity, and the king asked him his favorite dish. "Partridge," the priest said, and the king ordered him to eat only partridge every day. "How were your meals?" the king asked after a few weeks, and the priest replied, "Very good, but partridge, always partridge." "Ah, yes," said the amorous king, "and one wife is all very well, but not 'partridge, always partridge!'"

Of the late brilliant lexicographer and etymologist Eric Partridge, an especially indefatigable worker who took on jobs few others would consider tackling, it was once said, "Partridge is always game."

PEACOCK

George III, during one of his attacks of insanity, insisted on ending every sentence in all of his speeches with the word *peacock*. His ministers cured him of this by telling him that *peacock* was a beautiful word but a royal one, which a king should whisper when speaking before his subjects so they couldn't hear it. As a result the speeches of George III were less absurd.

PECUNIARY

Pecu is the Latin word for cattle, and since cattle were a common means of barter at the time, the ancients often expressed the value of an estate in terms of the number of cattle it was valued at, which gave them the word *pecunia,* for money or property. *Pecunia* gave rise to a number of English words, some of them obsolete now, like *pecuny* ("money"), but many still thriving, such as *pecuniary,* "pertaining to money"; *impecunious,* "without money"; *peculate,* "to embezzle"; and *peculiar,* "pertaining to that which is one's own," that is, one's own cattle.

Similarly, the Old English *feoh* ("cattle"), which is a cognate of the Latin *pecu,* gave us the word *fee,* cattle again coming to mean money.

PEDIGREE

—a three-line symbol used by medieval genealogists in denoting the line of descent of families they were tracing—was thought by some observant scholar to resemble the imprint of the bony foot of a crane. In French, the court language in many kingdoms, "foot of the crane" was *pied de grue,* which came to be both the name for the genealogical symbol and the name for the line or genealogical table itself. Introduced into English in the fifteenth century, *pied de grue* became through distorted spelling *pee de grew, petiegrew,* and *peti degree,* among many other versions, before settling down here as *pedigree.*

PETRELS

Stormy petrels take their name from the way the birds seem to be patting the waves with one foot and then the other in stormy weather, as though they were walking on the water. Actually they are flying close to the waves in search of surface-swimming food like small shrimp, but the birds reminded sailors of St. Peter walking upon the Lake of Gennesaret to join Jesus (Matthew 14:29). They were thus named *peterels,* a diminutive of the English *Peter,* in honor of the apostle, and this came to be *petrel* in time. All petrels are regarded as the protectors of sailors and the harbingers of approaching storms. It is considered bad luck to kill one, for the birds were long thought to be the souls of drowned and shipwrecked men, and whenever one died sailors believed a crew member would soon die to take its place.

How petrels got the nickname *Mother Carey's chickens* is a mystery. No real Mother Carey has been found, many etymologists upholding Brewer's theory that the words are a corruption of the Latin *Mater Cara* (Dear Mother), another name for the Virgin Mary. However, in the absence of evidence, Ernest Weekley's conclusion in *The Romance of Words* still seems best: "Mother Carey's chicken, probably a nautical corruption of some old Spanish or Italian name; but, in spite of ingenious guesses, this lady's genealogy remains as obscure as that of Davy Jones or the Jolly Roger."

TO PIGEONHOLE

The expression originated in the mid-nineteenth century. At the time side-by-side compartments in old-fashioned rolltop desks were called *pigeonholes* because of their resemblance to the holes in dovecotes, or pigeon houses, which were made to enable pigeons to walk in and out. Since papers were filed in these compartments, *to pigeonhole* became a way of saying to file away for future reference. But papers filed away in pigeonholes were often ignored purposely because they presented a problem or the prospect of too much work, so the term *to pigeonhole* was humorously extended to mean filing something away with the intention of forgetting about it or doing nothing about it.

PIGGY BANKS

Piggy banks are not so named because they are made in the image of pigs—not entirely, anyway. In medieval times one meaning of *pig* or *pygg* was "an earthenware pot, pitcher, jar, or crock," *pig* or *pygg* having been a word for clay. Housewives often saved small coins in these earthenware containers, but it wasn't until the nineteenth century that some unknown potters got the idea to make one in the shape of a pig, like its coincidental namesake. The pig or pygg in the shape of a pig became so popular and commonplace that today its name is applied to any small bank for saving coins, whether it is shaped like a pig or not.

PIG LATIN

Ixnay (nix, no), *amscray* (scram), and several other slang words come to us directly from *pig Latin*. First known as *dog Latin,* the little language commonly used by schoolchildren can be traced back to at least mid-eighteenth-century England, when there was a *dog Greek* as well as a *dog Latin.* The *dog* in the term means the same as it does in *doggerel,* something bad, spurious, bastard, mongrel. *Dog Latin* probably came to be called *pig Latin* and *hog Latin* because its sound resembles the grunting of hogs.

The lopped language was at first a combination of Latin and English. Today it is basically formed by taking the first letter of a word, putting it at the rear of the word and adding an *ay* to it. For example, "You can talk pig Latin" is "Ouyay ankay alktay igpay Atinlay." One interesting pig Latin word is *ofay,* a derogatory term blacks in Chicago originated for a white person, which is said to be pig Latin for the word *foe.*

Pig Latin is much easier to decipher on paper than when the gibberish of words is heard in conversation, thus it has always been popular as a code or secret language.

TO PLAY CAT AND MOUSE WITH

Surprisingly enough, feminists arrested during the suffragette agitation in England in about 1913 inspired the first popular use of this expression. The suffragettes often went on hunger strikes when imprisoned, and the government retaliated by passing the "Prisoners' Temporary Discharge for Ill-Health Act," which said that prisoners could be set free while fasting but were liable for rearrest when they recovered from their fasts to serve the remainder of their sentences. Critics compared the government's action to a big cat cruelly playing with a little mouse and dubbed the legislation "The Cat and Mouse Act." From the act, which wasn't particularly successful, came the popularization of *to play cat and mouse with,* though the expression may have been used long before this.

171

TO PLAY POSSUM

Oppossum is one of the earliest of Americanisms. Borrowed from Indian language, it made its first appearance as *oppossoun* in 1610, was changed to *opassom* a few years later, and within a century was being written as *oppossum* and its abbreviated form *possum*. The animal, which Captain John Smith described as having "an head like a swine, a taile like a rat, and is of the bigness of a cat," was known from colonial times for the way it feigned death when threatened with capture. Trapped possums close their eyes and lie completely limp; no matter how much abuse they are subjected to, they will only become active when thrown into water. Hunters have known this from the earliest days, and so although the expression *to play possum,* to pretend or deceive, was first recorded in 1822, the phrase is probably much older. Why the saying has never had anything to do with the futility or stupidity of the possum's ploy is a mystery—unless it was widely known that the possum plays dead because many predators won't eat animals they haven't killed themselves.

TO PLAY THE SEDULOUS APE

Robert Louis Stevenson originated the phrase in a charming essay where he wrote: "I have played the sedulous ape to Hazlitt, to Lamb, to Wordsworth, to Sir Thomas Browne, to Defoe, to Hawthorne, to Montaigne, to Baudelaire, and to Obermann. . . . That, like it or not, is the way to learn to write." *Sedulous,* from the Latin *sedulus,* care-

172

ful, means diligent and persevering in application or attention, so the phrase describes anyone who slavishly imitates somebody.

POLITICAL ELEPHANTS
AND DONKEYS

Cartoonist Thomas Nast is supposed to have invented the symbols of both the Republican and Democratic parties. In an 1874 *Harper's Weekly* Nast drew a cartoon in which an elephant is labeled "The Republican Vote." In 1879 he did another cartoon for the same magazine showing an elephant labeled "Republican Party" and a donkey labeled "Democratic Party." But in 1848 the Whig paper *Field Piece* several times showed a donkey in cartoons with the label "Democratic platform."

PONGO

The *pongo* was "a cross between a tiger and a sea-shark," a terrible monster that devastated Sicily until it was slain by the three sons of St. George, according to medieval legend. By a strange coincidence the word is the name in an Angolan dialect for a large anthropoid ape, either a gorilla or a chimpanzee. For this reason early explorers called these apes pongos beginning in the seventeenth century and continued using the word frequently for some three hundred years, even applying it to the orangutan. Today the once common word is not even found in most dictionaries.

PONY, PONY EXPRESS

Would you believe that the pony is related to the young chicken? It is, but only in language. Both words have their roots in the Latin word *pullus,* "a young animal," which yielded the French *poulet,* "a young fowl," this becoming the English *pullet* and the French *poulenet,* "a young horse," which became the Scottish *powney* and then the English *pony.*

The *Pony Express,* more often called simply the *Pony* at the time, was the common designation for the Central Overland Pony Express Company, which lasted only from April 3, 1860, to October 24, 1861, but is still operating in Western novels and films. It had 190 stations along its route between Missouri and California, riders including "Buffalo Bill" Cody, changing swift Indian ponies at each station and riding on with the mail—often through bad weather and Indian ambushes. The record for its 2000-mile run was seven days, seventeen hours, but it couldn't beat the telegraph that connected East and West in 1861, and went out of business that year.

TO PONY UP

To pony up or *poney up* has been American slang for to pay up since about 1824. The simplest explanation is that it derives from the German *ponieren,* "to pay." But *pony* was British slang for a small amount of money in the early nineteenth century—probably because a pony is a small horse (not over fourteen and a half hands high)—and the term *to pony up* probably derived from this expression. Other uses of *pony* to indicate smallness include the pony that is a small glass of liquor, the pony describing a small book or magazine, and the small, pony chorus girl.

PORK BARREL

Government appropriations used to supply funds for local improvements that are designed to ingratiate congressmen with their constituents have been called *pork barrel* since shortly after the Civil War. Before that the term simply meant the total amount of contributions to a congressman's campaign fund. *Pork* in this case is synonymous with fat, which has always signified abundance or plenty. Political pork has an infinite variety of disguises: local federal buildings, roads, dams, the list goes on and on. Pork barrel is often of little benefit to the nation as a whole, but this isn't always the case. The Rivers and Harbors Bill has traditionally been the legislation loaded with the greatest number of those pet projects of congressmen seeking to reward their supporters in the hope of retaining their support and winning reelection.

POTSHOT

Hunters who killed game without any regard for rules of sportsmanship, who killed simply to fill the cooking pot back home, were reproachfully called *potshot* hunters in the sixteenth century. Their potshots, fired at young animals out of season, at birds on the ground, and so on, came in time to mean any indiscriminate shot fired at an animal or person who has no chance to escape or defend himself.

PUG-NOSED

In the seventeenth century *pug,* which derives from *puck,* a term of endearment, was a pet name for both apes and a popular short-haired dog. Both apes and the pug dog have blunt, snub noses with wide bases that slope upward, which inspired some wag to dub similar human noses *pug noses.* Students of physiognomy believed that a pug nose was an indication of weakness; even Emerson wrote that "a squint, a pug-nose, mats of hair . . . betray character." In fact, Charles Darwin had a snub nose, and Captain Fitzhugh of the *Beagle,* a devotee of the "science," almost didn't hire him as the ship's naturalist because a snub nose was supposed to indicate a lack of energy or determination.

PUMPERNICKEL

When in Germany, Napoleon's groom was supposedly offered a slice of coarse, dark rye bread and indignantly refused it, saying that it was fit only for the emperor's horse, Nickel. *C'est du pain pour Nickel,* the gourmet groom protested ("It is bread for Nickel"), and *pain pour Nickel* stuck as the name for the bread. But most scholars don't appreciate this ingenious story, which has the German bread named after a horse, though for once they do offer an interesting tale in exchange. *Webster's New Twentieth Century Dictionary of the English Language* and other authorities derive *pumpernickel* from the German *pumpern* ("to break wind") and *Nickel* ("a goblin or the devil"), inferring that pumpernickel is so named because it made people who ate it "break wind like the devil."

TO PUSSYFOOT AROUND

Teddy Roosevelt seems to have either coined or popularized the word *pussyfoot* in about 1905. Meaning crafty, cunning, or moving in a cautious manner, it refers to the way cats can walk stealthily by drawing in their claws and walking on the pads of their feet. It's very unlikely that the redoubtable William Eugene "Pussyfoot" Johnson, a crusading American do-gooder, had anything to do with the expression. Johnson was nicknamed Pussyfoot because of his catlike methods in tracking down lawbreakers when he served as chief special officer in the Indian Territory, from 1908 to 1911. Later his nickname in the form of *pussyfooters* was applied to all advocates of prohibition. While crusading in England, fresh from his triumph of securing the passage of prohibition here, Johnson was blinded by a stone thrown by a crusading drunk.

TO PUT THE CART
BEFORE THE HORSE

When Cicero said these words in 61 B.C. they were already proverbial. Actually, their Latin version, literally translated, means "the plow draws the ox in reversed position," but it conveys the same idea; that is, to get things in the reverse or wrong order. The Roman proverb was first translated into English in 1279, and over the years the ox became a horse and the plow a cart. The proverb is ancient in French, German, and Italian as well as English. Our word *preposterous* conveys a similar idea. It is from the Latin *prae*, "before," and *posterus*, "after," and freely translated means "the before coming after," which sug-

177

gests its meaning of nonsensical or absurd. Sometimes carts *were* legitimately put before horses, as when horses pushed empty carts into coal mines.

PUTTING ON THE DOG

Lapdogs were all the rage among the new rich in America shortly after the Civil War, especially King Charles and Blenheim spaniels, rather imperious-looking dogs to the common man and certainly very distant relatives sociologically of the average American mutt, who had to work or scrounge for his supper. These snooty dogs being pampered by their snooty owners probably inspired the expression *putting on the dog,* showing off, which apparently arose in the 1860s as college slang at Yale University. Attempts to derive *put on the dog* from the older *put on side* all seem strained. The reasoning behind the latter is that dogs "show off" by arching out one side while moving their feet in intricate maneuvers.

PYTHON

The Greek verb meaning "to rot" is the word from which *python* is derived, not a likely source for the name of the largest living snake next to the anaconda. The first Python was a huge serpent slain near Delphi by Apollo, and the monster rotted in the sun after it died. The name of the mythological serpent wasn't given to real snakes until 1836, though it had been applied in English to other mythical monsters two centuries before this.

Q

The Phoenicians may have originally based this letter upon a monkey with its tail hanging down.

QUAIL

Sometimes *quail* is still used as slang for a woman, much like *bird* in England, but it once meant a courtesan or prostitute. It took this meaning because, as Eric Partridge noted, the quail was thought to be a bird of "an inordinately amorous disposition."

QUARRY

Although the *quarry* is now the object of any chase—the deer in hunting, the bird flown at in falconry—it once meant something entirely different. In the Middle Ages the quarry, the word deriving from the Latin *corium,* "skin," was the entrails of the deer placed on the animal's skin as a reward for the hounds after a hunt.

QUARTER HORSES

Quarter horses are so named for their ability to run well in quarter-mile races, not because of their lineage. The term is an Americanism, first recorded in 1834, though *quarter races* are mentioned a good fifty years earlier as being very popular in the South. Quarter horses, usually smaller than longer-distance-race horses, were also called *quarter nags.*

R (THE DOG LETTER)

Those who pronounce Harvard *Hahvad* won't find any precedent in the traditional pronunciation of the letter *R*. Since Roman times *R* has been thought of as the *dog's letter,* or the snarling letter, because its sound resembles the snarling of a dog—*r-r-r-r.* Ben Jonson, in his *English Grammar Made for the Benefit of All Strangers* (1636), put it this way: "R is the dog's letter, and hurreth in the sound; the tongue striking the inner palate, with a trembling about the teeth." Shakespeare has Juliet's nurse in *Romeo and Juliet* call *R* the *dog-name,* when she tells Romeo that his name and rosemary, an herb associated with weddings, both begin with an *R*. In parts of America, especially the Midwest, *R* is still pronounced as the dog letter, while in other regions, particularly parts of New England and the South, it is sounded as *ah.*

RAINING CATS AND DOGS

The only literal explanation for *raining cats and dogs* is that during heavy rains in seventeenth-century England some city streets became raging rivers of filth carrying many dead cats and dogs. The first printed use of the phrase does date to the seventeenth century, when English playwright Richard Brome wrote in *The City Witt* (1652): "It shall rain dogs and polecats." His use of "polecats" certainly suggests a less literal explanation, but no better theory has been offered. Other conjectures are that the hyperbole comes from a Greek saying, similar in sound, meaning "an unlikely occurrence," and that the phrase derives from a rare French word, *catadoupe* ("a waterfall"), which sounds a little like *cats and dogs*. It could also be that the expression was inspired by the fact that cats and dogs were closely associated with the rain and wind in northern mythology, dogs often pictured as the attendants of Odin, the storm god, and cats believed to cause storms. Similar colloquial expressions include *it's raining pitchforks, darning needles, hammer handles,* and *chicken coops.*

RARA AVIS

A rare person or thing, someone out of the ordinary, a rare bird. *Rara avis* is the Latin for a rare bird, and the expression was first used figuratively by the Roman satirist Juvenal. "A bird rarely seen on earth, and very like a black swan," Juvenal called one of his fellow Romans (*Rara avis in terris nigroque simillima cygno*). He chose a black swan for his comparison although black swans, native to Australia, were unknown at the time.

RED HERRING

Red herring are simply herring that have been cured and become red in color. So strong is their smell that seventeenth-century sportsmen sometimes used them to train hound dogs when the dogs didn't respond to the scent of a dead fox or cat that had been dragged along a trail. But British criminals soon learned that the scent of a red herring served to divert a dog as well as train him, that dragging a red herring across a trail would make a blood-hound lose the human scent he'd been following. From this practice of "faulting the hounds" came the expression *to drag* (or *draw*) *a red herring across the trail* (and the more recent truncated term *red herring*), which means evading an issue by dragging in something irrelevant to the matter, using any device to confuse or divert attention from the real question at hand.

REMORA

Remora, ranging in size from seven to thirty-six inches, make their way about the ocean by attaching themselves upside down to the undersides of sharks; some species are found on whales, swordfish, and tuna as well. The shark remora (*Remora remora*) attaches itself by means of its highly efficient suction disk, which is a greatly modified first and spiny dorsal fin. This remora not only hitches a free ride but eats pieces of food dropped by the shark. It may, nevertheless, do some good, because scientists be-lieve it possibly acts as a cleaner fish, removing parasites from the shark's hide. The Romans, however, thought the little parasite was worthless, believing that it fastened itself

183

to their sailing vessels and slowed them down, delaying them. Therefore they named the fish the *remora,* "the delayer."

REQUIEM SHARK

There is an interesting story about the French word *requin,* for shark, one that is best told in the words of the pseudonymous Sinbad, who recorded it in *Sharks, Sea and Land* (1887):

> The French name for shark is *requin.* This word is probably derived from the Latin *requiem,* and signifies that if a man fall into the sea among sharks, his comrades may repeat for him the usual prayers for the dead. It is seldom, if ever, that a man who is so luckless as to fall amongst sharks appears again; a shriek is heard, a moving mass is seen under the surface and a fin above it; the next wave that breaks against the shipside is crimsoned, and the horror-stricken seamen know that their messmate has gone to that place from which no traveler returns.

I should add that the tiger shark and other tropical sharks of the family Carcharhinidae are called requiem sharks, probably for the same reason. (See also *Shark.*)

RHINOCEROS

As with the hippopotamus (*q.v.*) and many other animals, the Greeks named the *rhinoceros.* They thought the huge horn on its head very formidable and called it *rhinokeros* after the Greek words *rhinos,* "nose," and *keras,* "horn."

The rhino's horn, sometimes over four feet long, is an excellent defensive weapon, but it has plagued the animal through the ages, driving it at times to the shores of the Dead Sea of extinction. One old canard had it that a rhino horn used as a goblet could detect the presence of poison; other superstitions claimed that powdered rhino horn could cure many ailments, including epilepsy and bubonic plague, as well as ease the pain of childbirth. Yet what caused the rhino the most trouble was the belief that its horn, similar to the legendary unicorn's, was a sex stimulant. The ancient Chinese, Babylonians, Greeks, and Romans were among many people who believed this. Today at least three species of rhino are becoming extinct because the Chinese value their powdered horn (*hsi chio*) as an aphrodisiac—a large horn brings at least $1,000 in what is definitely a seller's market.

American chemists claim that rhino horn powder contains no magic substance that could be classed as an aphrodisiac, and Britain's Prince Philip, Queen Elizabeth's consort, once denounced it as "useless," telling an audience of eastern diplomats and ambassadors that the belief that rhino horn is a potent aphrodisiac "is complete poppycock—a laughable travesty of the truth." This, however, did little to change the tactics of the millions in the Far East and Africa who believe "the magic powder" to be the most powerful sex stimulant known to humanity. In some places powdered rhino horn is literally worth its weight in gold, and in London alone a million dollars' worth of the substance, mostly from South Africa, is auctioned off each year. Two hundred rhinos must die to produce that much powder, but protective measures have only succeeded in forcing the price still higher. They have also prompted some strange poaching cases. Several years ago, for example, thieves broke into a natural history museum in Jakarta, Indonesia, and sawed the horns off seven stuffed rhino heads.

Both the black and the white rhinoceros species of Africa are misnamed, for both of them are slate gray in color. The white rhino, in fact, may have taken its first name from the Dutch *wijd*, "wide," for its wide upper lip and muzzle, this corrupted to *white* over the years.

TO RIDE ROUGHSHOD OVER

A roughshod horse had nail heads projecting from its shoes to keep it from slipping, and it is said that similar shoes with projecting points were designed by blacksmiths in the seventeenth century for use by the cavalry on the battlefield. The gory spectacle of chargers with nailed hooves stomping over men in the battle, or even the sight of a roughshod horse accidentally trampling a pedestrian on a city street, suggested the expression *to ride rough- shod over* someone, to treat someone brutally, without the least consideration.

ROBIN, ROBIN REDBREAST

There are no true American robins, the bird we call a *robin* (*Turdus migratorius*) actually being a thrush. Our "robin" takes its name from *robin redbreast,* the British name for another bird species. According to tradition a robin pulled a thorn from Christ's crown on the way to Calvary, and the blood spurting from the wound dyed the robin's breast red forever.

TO RULE THE ROOST

There's no doubt that this expression is well over four centuries old, but there is much controversy over whether it was originally *to rule the roost* or *to rule the roast*. To rule the roost would of course refer to the cock who rules the chicken coop and to rule the roast refers to the lord of the manor who presided over the carving of roast meat at the table and was thus master of the house. Americans still prefer the former expression and the British use the latter. Since early references are found for both versions, the truth will probably never be known. What complicates matters impossibly is that *roost* was formerly pronounced as we now pronounce *roast,* and thus spelled *roast* erroneously, while *roast* was sometimes pronounced *roost* and spelled that way. In any case, the expression means the same—to rule the house or whatever, usually while making a display of power.

TO RUN RIOT

The Master of Game, a hunting manual published in 1410, explains in part that *to run riot* was originally a term describing a hunting dog who lost the scent of the animal he was chasing and began acting unruly and undisciplined—running after other animals instead of the intended quarry. Over the next century the phrase came to be used figuratively for anyone acting without constraint or control.

SACRED COW

The Hindu hero Prithvi changed himself into a cow to encourage his countrymen to be vegetarians. This and the doctrine of *ahimsa,* harmlessness to all living things, preached by Buddha, account for the fact that cows are still sacred in India, roaming the streets at will. Our fairly recent term *sacred cow,* any person or group so highly regarded as to be exempt from even justified criticism, appears to stem from the Hindu belief. It probably came into the language when Mahatma Gandhi's passive resistance movement brought worldwide attention to India. Gandhi himself was a confirmed vegetarian. In his youth he did try eating meat but gave it up when he had recurring nightmares of animals bleeding in his stomach.

SALMONELLA

Salmon have no connection with *Salmonella* or *salmonellosis*. The latter is a very common form of food poisoning that can result in death and is caused by bacteria of the *Salmonella* genus, comprising some fifteen hundred species. The *Salmonella* genus was first identified by nineteenth-century American pathologist and veterinarian Daniel Elmer Salmon, who died in 1914. There are often outbreaks of salmonellosis, which is usually caused by infected and insufficiently cooked beef, pork, poultry, and eggs, as well as food, drink, or equipment contaminated by the excreta of infected animals. Nearly all animals are hospitable to the rod-shaped bacteria causing the acute gastroenteritis in humans, and food poisonings caused by them are almost as common as those caused by staphylococci. Incidentally, there is a "salmon disease" dogs and other animals get from eating salmon infested with cysts of flukes—it has nothing to do with salmonellosis. *Salmonella,* some experts fear, could become an "Andromeda strain." It seems that generations of livestock raised for human consumption have been fed miracle drugs for so long that they have developed races of bacteria that are immune to the germ-killing properties of antibiotics. These *Salmonella* could be passed on to the consumer, infecting humans in epidemic proportions with a salmonellosis antibiotics would be powerless against. The theory is highly controversial, but the FDA considers it likely enough to be conducting extensive investigations at this writing.

SCARCER THAN HEN'S TEETH

Nothing is *scarcer than hen's teeth* because not even Ripley has ever found a hen with even a single tooth. The Americanism, which also means nonexistent, probably goes back to colonial days, though it was first recorded in 1862.

TO SEE RED

To see red, to be roused to violent anger, comes from the older saying *to wave a red flag at a bull.* The expression became popular in America during this century, deriving of course from the waving of a red cape to rouse the bull in bullfights. No matter that bulls are color-blind, that only the brightness and waving of the cape arouses them. The misconception is so widespread and red is so universally associated with violence that the words will be with us long after bullfighting is banned.

A SERPENT IN ONE'S BOSOM

Legend says a Greek shepherd found a frozen serpent and put it under his shirt. The snake revived but bit its benefactor, which gives us this saying for an ungrateful person.

SERPENT-LICKED EARS

Those with *serpent-licked ears,* should any horseplayer want to try, are said to have the power of seeing into the future. The ancient Greeks believed that both Cassandra and Helenus had the power of prophecy because serpents licked their ears while they slept in the temple of Apollo.

SHARK

Sharks of the sea take their name from land sharks, rather than the other way around, which is the usual order of things. *Shark* derives from the German *schurke,* "a greedy parasite," and German sailors applied the word to the sea creature with the land shark in mind. English sailors brought the word back to England in about 1569, the year John Hawkins, the first English mariner engaged in the African slave trade, exhibited a huge shark in London. The word was quickly adopted to describe the "killer fish" and is first recorded some thirty years later in English to describe his human counterpart.

SHREWD

A *shrewd* person several centuries ago was someone evil, vicious, and extremely dangerous. The word most likely comes from the name of the shrew, a small mouselike animal with a long snout common in the forests of England. Shrews are extremely truculent animals, which will often fight to the death over a bit of food, the victor eating the loser in the bargain. An old superstition held them to be poisonous as well. Thus a *shrew* became an evil, vicious person, especially a woman who scolded or nagged, as in Shakespeare's *The Taming of the Shrew,* and the verb *to shrew* formed from this noun gave us the word *shrewd* in its past participle. Over the centuries shrewd lost its meaning of evil but retained the qualities of sharpness and cleverness that made the little shrew formidably wicked, so that today shrewd means keen-witted, clever, sharp in practical affairs.

SILLY AS A COOT

The coot's facial expression and clownish behavior inspired the expressions *silly as a coot, stupid as a coot,* and *crazy as a coot.* During the breeding season *Fulica americana* acts especially odd, according to *Birds of Sea, Shore and Stream,* "breaking water, flapping wings, sitting on their tails, slashing at one another with taloned feet, and thrusting with their bills. They further vent their feelings in explosive cacks, clucks, coos, and wails." The first recorded use of *coot* for a bald person, as in *an old coot,* recorded in 1430, refers to the waterfowl's forehead, upon which is formed a bald patch when its bill is raised.

TO SING LIKE A CANARY

Canaries are named for dogs. It happened that in about 40 B.C. Juba, the native chief of Mauritania, explored a group of islands far off the coast of his kingdom and named the largest of them Canaria, or "Island of Dogs," because of the wild dogs inhabiting it. Later visitors called the whole island group the Canary Islands, and when the grayish-green songbird of the island was tamed and exported in the sixteenth century, it became widely known as "the bird from the Canary Islands," which was inevitably shortened to *canary*. It took years of selective breeding to produce yellow canaries; much of the breeding was done in Germany, where the best singing canaries were also bred—these called Harz Mountain canaries. Informants or stool pigeons are sometimes said by police *to sing like a canary* when they reveal everything they know.

SKUNK

Because the little striped mammal could squirt his foul yellow spray up to twelve feet, American Indians called him *segankw,* or *segonku,* the Algonquian dialect word meaning simply "he who squirts." Early pioneers corrupted the hard-to-pronounce Algonquian word to *skunk,* and that way it has remained since. Today we know the skunk's foul spray as m-butyl mercaptan, or $CH_3C_2CH_2CH_2SH$, but it smells as bad under any name. The skunk was called *enfant du diable,* "child of the devil," by French-Canadian trappers, but it is also called the wood polecat and wood pussy. The most common species is the striped skunk, *Mephitis mephitis,* which might be loosely translated as "doubly stinky," though *mephitis* means a noxious exhalation from the ground.

SLOTHFUL

The name of the animal in this case did not give us the words *sloth* and *slothful,* as several sources indicate. *Sloth,* deriving from the Middle English *slou,* "slow," dates back to at least 1175 as a word for laziness and the adjective slothful is recorded as early as 1390. The arboreal mammal of South America called the sloth didn't get its name until the early nineteenth century. The sloth does virtually nothing for weeks on end, not breathing for long periods, taking at least two weeks to digest its food, and not even springing up if it falls out of its tree. It was named by explorers who observed it, one telling of how a sloth took "three or four days at least, in climbing up and down a tree," and another observing that one took "a whole day in going fifty paces."

SLOW AND STEADY WINS THE RACE

Charles Darwin measured the speed of a Galápagos turtle by walking beside it and found that it "walked at the rate of sixty yards in ten minutes, that is 360 yards in an hour, or four miles a day,—allowing a little time for it to eat on the road." That is certainly slow enough for an expression *slow as a tortoise,* but the creature, unlike the snail, has been noted for his reliability rather than his lack of speed. The expression *slow and steady wins the race* is from the poem "The Hare and the Tortoise" by Robert Lloyd (1733–1764) but can be traced back in all but its exact form to Aesop's fable "The Hare and the Tortoise," in which the hare awakens to see the tortoise crossing the finish line in a race the hare was sure he would win.

SMALL FRY

Fry are the progeny of salmon, herring, and other fish, the word deriving from the Norse *frae,* "seed," which first described the berry- or seedlike masses of eggs these fish produce. Many people think that *small fry* for young children is a fairly recent invention referring to young fish, but fry was used this way almost from the time it was introduced into English and even small fry used figuratively dates back to 1697. Harriet Beecher Stowe employed small fry ("smaller fry") to describe children in *Uncle Tom's Cabin.*

A SNAIL'S PACE

For the record, a snail's pace is usually from twenty-three inches to fifty-five yards per hour, depending on the species, though a snail may move as little as an inch every three weeks. As one would suspect, the phrase *a snail's pace* goes far back in the language, first recorded in about 1400, and references to the snail's slowness date back even further. An old variant on the words is *a snail's gallop.* A snail moves along by secreting a layer of mucus so that it can glide over any surface, no matter how rugged, the retractable foot on its body so tough that it can crawl across the edge of a sharp razor without cutting itself. The slowpoke is strong, too. Snail species only half an ounce in weight can drag more than a pound of weight over a smooth surface—which is equivalent to a man of 200 pounds pulling over three tons. No wonder snails have considerable self-esteem and build themselves castles, even though they don't get where they're going as quick as a wink of your winkpeepers—that being ".3 second to .4 second," according to Pedler's *Physiology of the Eye.*

A SNAKE IN THE GRASS

Latet anguis in herba (a snake lurks in the grass), the Roman poet Virgil wrote in the third *Eclogue,* and from this ancient source comes our common expression for a hidden or hypocritical enemy. Proving that times don't change much, the Latin proverb first appears in English as a line in a political song of about 1290: "Though all appears clean, a snake lurks in the grass."

SNUG AS A BUG IN A RUG

This phrase denotes the utmost in contentment. It is the latest and coziest of several phrases that have valiantly served before it: the Shakespearean *snug as a dog in a rug, snug as pigs in peas-straw* (1603), and *safe as a bug in a rug.* The southern American *happy as a dead pig in the sunshine* came much later.

SOUR GRAPES

In Aesop's fable "The Fox and the Grapes," a fox spied luscious-looking grapes hanging from a vine. Everyone knows that he leaped a number of times trying to get them, failing by a few inches with each leap, and gave up after rationalizing that they were probably sour and inedible anyway. La Fontaine, another great fabulist, later regarded the fox as admirable, remarking that his words were "better than complaining," but the fox's "sour grapes" have come to mean any belittling, envious remark.

SPANIEL

Shakespeare has Antony speak of the "hearts that spaniel'd me at heels, to whom I gave their wishes." *Spaniel* can be a verb and adjective, signifying affectionate humility, as well as a noun. The dog's name simply means "Spanish dog," deriving from the old French *chien espagneul,* which was shortened to *espagnol,* Spanish, and then *spaniel* in English. Either the spaniel was a breed developed in Spain or the dog reminded Europeans of the Spaniards, who were regarded as submissive and fawning during the Middle Ages. Neither the Spaniards nor the dog is servile, but the breed's silky hair and soft, soulful eyes may have suggested the appearance of the Spaniards. There is no hard evidence for this, however. The cocker spaniel gets his first name from the way he cocks his long, drooping ears, or possibly because he was trained to retrieve woodcocks.

SQUIRREL

The Greeks were impressed not so much by this bright-eyed rodent's acrobatic performances in trees as by its bushy tail, which they believed the animal wrapped around itself like a parasol when the sun was too strong. So they named the animal *skiouros*, "shadow tail," from their words for shade, *skia*, and tail, *oura*, meaning "shady tail, the animal that makes shade with its tail." The allusion was pleasant and poetic, but the road to our word *squirrel* was difficult. *Skiouros* became *sciurus* in Latin and then *esquireul* in French before going through nearly a score of English spellings and becoming the squirrel that we know today.

STARLING

The starling (*Sturnus vulgaris*) deserves some space here because it constitutes more of the 100 billion birds in the world than any other species. The bird has been noted for its ability to speak and whistle, Shakespeare mentioning a starling in *Henry IV*, Part I, "taught to speake nothing but 'Mortimer.' " The bird, whose name is akin to the Old English for tern, *stearn*, was brought across the Atlantic and released in Central Park in 1890 by literary enthusiasts seeking to introduce all the birds mentioned in Shakespeare to America. It has since become something of a pest, reminding some gardeners of the Englishman back in 1886 who said, "Few people are aware of how good the starling is to eat."

TO START FROM SCRATCH

Unlike *to come up to scratch*, which probably derives from prizefighting, these words were originally horse racing slang. A *scratch* in England was the starting line in a horse race and horses started there with no advantage besides their own ability, like anyone who starts from scratch in any undertaking. In this sense a *scratch race* is one without restrictions as to the age, weight, and winnings of the horses entered. *To scratch* a horse from a race has entirely different origins, resulting from a race official crossing a horse's name off the entry list.

STATE ANIMALS

In the past many of the animal nicknames below for state inhabitants were widely used nationally, but today they haven't much currency. Several are the nicknames of state university football teams (Badgers, Wolverines), but not because they are associated with state residents. Most state residents describe themselves as New Yorkers, Mainers, Nebraskans, Californians, and the like, but in case something more colorful is needed, this selected state list is historically accurate. Some of the names aren't very complimentary and were obviously bestowed by residents of other states. A similar list could be made of nicknames of the residents of cities, with humorous examples like *Omahogs;* and the name Walter Winchell gave Chicago gangsters, *Chicagorillas.*

> Alabama—yellowhammers, lizards
> Delaware—muskrats, blue hen's chickens
> Florida—alligators, gators
> Georgia—buzzards
> Illinois—suckers
> Iowa—hawkeyes
> Kansas—grasshoppers, jayhawkers
> Kentucky—bears, red horses
> Louisiana—pelicans
> Maine—foxes

Maryland—clam humpers, craw thumpers, oysters
Michigan, "the Wolverine State"—wolverines
Minnesota, "the Gopher State"—gophers
Mississippi—mud cats, tadpoles
Nebraska—bug eaters
Nevada—sage hens
New Jersey—clams, clam catchers
Oregon, "the Beaver State"—beavers
South Carolina—ricebirds, weasels
South Dakota, "the Coyote State"—coyotes
Tennessee—whelps, buckskins
Texas—beef heads, longhorns
Utah, "The Beehive State"—bees
Virginia—beagles
Washington—clam grabbers
Wisconsin, "the Badger State"—badgers
Wyoming—sheep herders

TO STAVE OFF

A *stave* is a stick of wood, the word a back formation from the plural of staff, *staves*. In the early seventeenth century staves were used in the "sport" of bullbaiting, where dogs were set against bulls. Too often these contests were badly matched, for the bulls usually had the tips of their horns cut off, and when the dogs got a bull down, the bull's owner often tried to save him for another fight by driving the dogs off with a stave or stick. Because the owner actually "postponed" the bull's death until another day, the expression *to stave off* acquired its present figurative meaning of to forestall.

ST. BERNARD

Men crossed the Alps between Switzerland and Italy centuries before St. Bernard de Menthon (923–1008) founded the shelter now called the Hospice of Great St. Bernard. But the house of refuge he built in 982 made it much easier for travelers to make pilgrimages to Rome through the Mons Jovis pass, 8,098 feet above sea level and covered with snow ten months of the year. St. Bernard, a wealthy French nobleman who renounced his fortune to become a man of God, was canonized in 1681. Perhaps two hundred years before this the monks at his hospice had begun breeding the great dogs that are named after him and training them to track down and rescue travelers lost in blizzards and avalanches. The breed is said to be a cross between a bulldog and a Pyrenean shepherd dog, or a Molossian hound, and it once had long hair believed to result from matings with the Newfoundland dog. The long hair was found to be a handicap in the snow, however, and a smooth-haired variety has been developed in relatively recent times. *St. Bernards* are still trained by the monks of the Alpine hospice. Measuring up to about six feet long, they are capable of carrying a man and are bred for intelligence and docility as well as strength. The breed is the world's heaviest dog, one specimen having reached a weight of 246 pounds. Numerous individual dogs have been honored as heroes, including the famous Barry, whose statue is in the St. Bernard Hospice. Barry saved the lives of forty travelers in ten years of heroic service. In one rescue he found a small boy unconscious in the snow, warmed the child with his breath, and licked his hands and face, rousing him from his deadly sleep. Then the dog managed to make the boy understand by movement and nudging that he wanted him to climb on his back, and carried him to safety.

St. Bernards of the Alpine hospice have never carried little kegs of brandy on their necks; a cartoon early in the 1900s is responsible for the myth.

STICK IN ONE'S CRAW

When you can't swallow something, when it won't go down with you or you are loath to accept it, it *sticks in your craw.* The craw is the crop or preliminary stomach of a fowl, where food is predigested. Hunters centuries ago noticed that some birds swallowed bits of stone that were too large to pass through the craw and into the digestive tract. These stones, unlike the sand and pebbles needed by birds to help grind food in the pouch, literally stuck in the craw, couldn't go down any farther. This oddity became part of the language of hunters and the phrase was soon used figuratively.

STOOL PIGEON

Only this expression remains of the billions of American passenger pigeons, once the most numerous birds ever to fly over the earth. Viciously cruel fowlers in the nineteenth century used live decoy birds to lure passenger pigeons into range of their nets or guns, which helped them to wipe out the species. These live decoys, their eyes sometimes stitched closed, or blinded by a needle stuck into their eyeballs, were called *stool pigeons,* probably because, among other methods, they were tied by a long string to small stools, which the hunters could move up and down while waiting hidden for their prey (although their name may derive from the Old English word *stale* meaning "a living bird used to catch others of the same species"). At any rate, in about 1830 the term stool pigeon became American slang for a criminal decoy used by the police to catch other criminals and by the end of the century it meant a police informer. The last meaning was probably influenced by the use of the slang *carrier pigeon* for an informer, a carrier pigeon carrying information to the police as the bird carries messages. *Stoolie,* an abbreviated form of the term, is of relatively recent usage. As for the passenger pigeon, the last one seen in the wild was shot by a boy with an air rifle on March 24, 1900, near Sargeants, Ohio, and can now be seen, stuffed, in the Smithsonian Institution.

STRAIGHT FROM THE HORSE'S MOUTH

By examining a horse's teeth an expert can make a good estimate of its age—a horse's first permanent teeth, for example, don't appear until it is about two and a half years old. So, despite what any crooked horse trader might have wished them to believe, informed horsemen in England stood little chance of being cheated about a horse's age— they had it on good authority, *straight from the horse's mouth.* The expression came into racetrack use in about 1830 and was part of everyday speech by 1900. (See also *Don't Look a Gift Horse in the Mouth.*)

THE STRAW THAT BROKE THE CAMEL'S BACK, LAST STRAW

Dickens appears to have invented these expressions in *Dombey and Son,* where he wrote: "As the last straw breaks the laden camel's back." But he got the idea from an old English proverb: " 'Tis the last feather that breaks the horse's back." Both phrases, of course, mean someone's limit or breaking point. I don't know about horses, but the strongest camel can carry 1,200 pounds—a straw more might literally break its back.

TO STRING ALONG

To string along means to accept someone's decision or advice, to follow someone as a leader, to go along with someone. In 1799 a political observer spoke of "the sycophantic circle that surrounds the President in stringing to his quarters." To string along probably comes from the same source as this earlier word, which suggests docile pack animals tied together in single file and led by their masters. The phrase isn't recorded until the 1920s.

SULKY

A *sulky,* a carriage pulled by a horse, seats only one person. Both the person in it and the horse drawing it often appeared aloof to old-timers. They humorously named the carriage after the driver and his horse, both of whom seemed sulky, appearing as if they wanted to be alone. The term, first recorded for a carriage in 1876, had previously been used to describe one-seated plows, cultivators, harnesses, and hay rakes.

SWAN SONG

Although the swan makes no utterance other than a hiss when it is angry, the ancient Greeks thought that the mute bird broke its lifelong silence with one last melodious song just before it died. The *swan song,* according to Socrates, was a happy one, for the dying bird, sacred to Apollo, knew that it would soon be joining the master it served. This superstition, embraced by poets through the ages, led to the use of swan song to mean a person's last, eloquent words or performance.

Shakespeare was called the Swan of Avon, Homer the Swan of Meander, and Virgil the Mantuan Swan because Apollo, the god of poetry and song, was fabled to have been changed into a swan and the souls of all poets were at one time thought to pass into the bodies of swans after death.

SWEETEN THE KITTY

In the game of faro the tiger was the bank or house, possibly because the tiger was once used on signs marking the entrance to Chinese gambling houses. Over the years gamblers transformed the tiger into a kitty, and it became the name for the pot in poker and other card games. By the end of the nineteenth century *sweeten* or *fatten the kitty* became a common expression for adding chips to the pot in a poker game or for increasing the payment in any business deal.

SWEETNESS AND LIGHT

Jonathan Swift invented this perennial phrase in his preface to the *Battle of the Books* (1704). Swift took the figure from the beehive when comparing the merits of the bee (the ancients) with the spider (the moderns): "The difference is that instead of dirt and poison, we have chosen to fill our hives with honey and wax, thus furnishing mankind with the two noblest things, which are sweetness and light." Later, Matthew Arnold, in *Culture and Anarchy* (1869), regarded these as the basic contribution of the artist and the basis of culture itself: "He who works for sweetness and light united, works to make reason and the will of God prevail."

TABBY CAT

Prince Attāb, the great grandson of Omeyua, famed in Arab legend, lived in a quarter of old Baghdad named *Attābiya* in his honor. Here a striped silk taffeta material was woven, the streaked fabric called *attabi* by the Arabs after the quarter, *attabi* eventually transformed to *tabis* in French during the Middle Ages and translated in English as *tabby cloth. Tabby* became a verb for to stripe soon after, and by 1695 the word was used to describe a brownish dark-striped or brindled *tabby cat* whose markings resembled the material. Old maids were also called *tabbies,* and this may have been because they often kept tabby cats and shared their careful habits, but the word for a spinster is more likely a pet form of *Tabitha.* Besides becoming a cloth, a cat, and possibly an old maid, Prince Attāb's name may have been used for the "falsies" that flat-chested girls wore in the eighteenth century, though these tabbies may have been suggested by tabs.

TADPOLE

An early spelling for *toad* was *tad,* and *pole* meant head in seventeenth-century speech. *Tadpole* therefore means toadhead, a good name for the early stage of a toad or frog when it is just a big head with a small tail. *Polliwog,* a synonym, comes from *pol,* head, and *wygle* (later corrupted in speech to *wog*), meaning "wigglehead."

TAKE THE BULL
BY THE HORNS

Since the earliest quotation yet found for this expression is from 1873, it seems unlikely that it has its roots in bull-running, a brutal English sport popular from the day of King John until it was outlawed in the mid-nineteenth century. Bull-running consisted of a mob with clubs and dogs chasing a bull loosed in the streets and eventually beating it to death, a favorite trick for the braver bull chasers being to grab the poor beast by the horns and wrestle it to the ground. More likely the expression originated in Spain or America. In bullfights, Spanish *banderilleros* plant darts in the neck of the bull and tire him more by waving cloaks in his face and seizing him by the horns, trying to hold his head down. Rawboned early ranchers in the American Southwest also wrestled bulls, or steers, in a popular sport called bulldogging that is still seen in rodeos—the object being to grab the animal's horns and throw him. Either of these practices could have prompted the saying *take the bull by the horns,* screw up your courage and cope with a dangerous or unpleasant situation decisively, head on.

TAKE UNDER ONE'S WING

This is a very old phrase, which was originally in the plural. It alludes, of course, to a hen protecting her chicks under her wings. The source for the phrase is biblical, the famous passage from Matthew 23:37: "O Jerusalem, Jerusalem, thou that killest the prophets, and stonest them which are sent unto thee, how often would I have gathered thy children together, even as a hen gathereth her chickens under her wings, and ye would not!"

TANTONY PIG

The smallest pig in a litter, one that is traditionally believed to follow its master anywhere, is called a *Tantony pig* after St. Anthony, long the patron saint of swineherds. St. Anthony probably had nothing to do with pigs, other than citing an "unclean demon" as one of the temptations he resisted, but he is often represented in art with a pig by his side. In the Middle Ages, when the pig began to lose its reputation as an unclean demon, it was popularly supposed that the animal was dedicated to the saint. St. Anthony, born about the year 250 in middle Egypt, defeated many "assaults by the devil," including temptations such as "gross and obscene imaginings" of beautiful, naked women that Lucifer sent to "harass him night and day," this particular temptation a favorite theme of medieval art. When his parents died St. Anthony gave his considerable inheritance to the poor, going to live in solitude for the great part of his life, and he is considered to be the first of the fraternity of ascetics who dwelt in the deserts. He is said to have died at age 105. The *Tantony bell*, a small hand bell or church bell, is also named for him, referring to the bell often depicted around his staff or the neck of his pig.

TARRED WITH THE SAME BRUSH

Someone who shares the sins or faults of another, though possibly to a lesser degree, is *tarred with the same brush*. The saying may have something to do with tarred and feathered criminals but the reference is more probably to the tarring of sheep. Owners of a flock of sheep, which, of course, can't be branded, used to mark their wool all in the same place with a brush dipped in tar to distinguish them from sheep of another flock. It is said that red ocher was used to make the mark and that brushing sheep with tar served to protect them against ticks.

TEDDY BEAR

Over sixty million *teddy bears* have been made since Brooklyn candy store owner Morris Michtom fashioned the first one out of brown plush in 1902 and named it after President Theodore Roosevelt. Michtom's inspiration was a cartoon by Washington *Post* cartoonist Clifford K. Berryman called "Drawing the Line in Mississippi," which had been reprinted throughout the country. Based on a news story about an expedition "Teddy" Roosevelt made to hunt bears near the Little Sunflower River in Mississippi, it showed the old Rough Rider with his back turned to a helpless bear cub. Gallant Teddy, it had been reported, refused to kill and even set free the small brown bear that his obliging hosts had stunned and tied to a tree for him to shoot. Apocryphal or not, the story enhanced Roosevelt's reputation as a conservationist and made Michtom rich. Roosevelt later presented a few bears to the Bronx Zoo, endearing himself more to arctophiles, and the teddy bear was still associated with him in 1911, when he received an honorary degree at Cambridge, England, and students lowered a large teddy bear onto his head from the ceiling while he stood on the platform. Our most energetic president was no slouch at coining words himself. *Muckraker, square deal, weasel word, nature faker, mollycoddle, big stick,* and *lunatic fringe* were all invented or revived and given new meaning by Teddy.

THERE'S A SUCKER BORN EVERY MINUTE

P. T. Barnum lived by this principle, but he probably didn't invent the phrase so often attributed to him. Since there is no recorded instance of Barnum uttering the words, they must be credited to "Anonymous," like another famous American cynicism, "Never give a sucker an even break," which was the title of a W. C. Fields movie about Barnum. The origin of the word *sucker* for a dupe or easily tricked person is a mystery as well. One theory holds that the slang word comes from the name of one of the many American freshwater fishes called suckers because they have lips that suggest that they feed by suction. Several of these fish are easily caught and might have suggested an easily hooked

211

or hoodwinked person. But the word, first recorded in 1831, could just as well derive from *sucker,* in the sense of a not-yet-weaned animal, the typical sucker's naiveté characteristic of a child still sucking at its mother's breast. Terms that Barnum did coin or help popularize include *Jumbo, bandwagon, Siamese twins, the Bearded Lady, the Wild Man of Borneo, Swedish Nightingale, Tom Thumb, Three-Ring Circus,* and *The Greatest Show on Earth.*

TILL THE COWS COME HOME

Relatively modern amplifications of this one include *Till the cows come home in the morning* and *Till hell freezes over and the cows come skating home over the ice.* The expression has meant a long, long time for a long, long time, since about 1600, and the idea behind it is that cows take their own good time about coming home if they aren't driven—often until the next morning, when, with udders painfully swollen, they come home to be milked.

TOADY

Some people still think that toads are deadly to eat, but in the seventeenth century this was a widespread belief. Audiences would oooh and ahhh when helpers of traveling medicine men ate toad legs and the charlatans promptly "cured" them with some worthless tonic that was then sold to the onlookers. These assistants became known as *toad-eaters,* and seemed so fawning—to the extent of eating "poisonous creatures" for their masters!—that their name in the corrupted form of *toady* became *the* word for a totally subservient person.

A TOWERING AMBITION

Towering in this phrase derives from a term in falconry. Castle watchtowers were the tallest structures in the Middle Ages, so high-flying hawks were said to tower. *Towering ambition* is thus ambition that is beyond ordinary bounds, as high as the towering of a hawk. *Towering rage* or *passion* could both be explained in the same way, rage or passion mounting to its highest point, but there is an added dimension that strengthens the phrases. When a falcon "towers" she hovers at the height of her ascent searching for prey, ready to swoop down in a murderous rage or passion on her victim.

TUNNEL

A *tonel* in the English of medieval times was a net with a wide mouth used to trap birds. From this word derived *tunnell* for the shaft of a chimney or any pipe or tube, which gave us the word *tunnel* for an underground passage.

TURKEY

The frankly stupid domesticated turkey hardly knows what to eat and has to be attracted to food by colorful marbles placed in its feed; it often catches cold by getting its feet wet and frequently panics and suffocates itself, when the flock presses together in fear. For such reasons *turkey* has been slang for any worthless, useless, unsuitable thing since before 1930. Since the early 1940s *turkey* has most often referred to a poorly done theatrical production that fails, sometimes called a *gobble*. Use of the word for a socially incompetent awkward person, a drip, fish, or square, dates back to the '40s, too, but has become increasingly popular recently and is possibly a reinvention from black street slang. In the past *turkey* has meant a coward, a fake drug capsule, easy money (because turkeys are comparatively easy to catch), an easy task (a turkey shoot), a valise, a fifty-cent piece (from the eagle on the coin), and a hobo's suitcase. *Irish turkey* is corned beef and cabbage. (See also *Let's Talk Turkey.*)

IN TWO SHAKES OF
A LAMB'S TAIL

A lamb can shake its tail twice quite rapidly, apparently before many animals can shake their tails once, which explains this Americanism meaning in hardly any time at all. The expression dates back to the early 1800s, and no one knows who invented it. Possibly it is a humorous extension of the older British phrase *in two shakes,* meaning the same and probably alluding to the quick shaking of a dice box in gambling.

UNDER THE AEGIS OF

The word *aigis* originally meant "goatskin" in Greek. Since Zeus, the Greeks' supreme deity, was suckled by the goat Amalthea and he used her skin or *aigis* to cover his shield, symbolic of his omnipotence, to be *under the aegis of* someone came to mean to be protected or supported by a great power.

UNDERDOG

The expression *underdog* appears to have originated in a popular nineteenth-century song by David Barker called "The Under Dog in the Fight." Two stanzas follow:

I know that the world, that the great big world,
   Will never a moment stop

To see which dog may be in the fault,
  But will shout for the dog on top.

But for me, I shall never pause to ask
  Which dog may be in the right,
For my heart will beat, while it beats at all,
  For the under dog in the fight.

URCHIN

What has the *street urchin,* a poor, mischievous, or roguish
child of the streets (not to mention the spiny *sea urchin*),
got to do with a hedgehog? All that happened was that the
English, who have almost invariably been poor at spelling
French words, stumbled badly over the synonym for
hedgehog that the Normans brought to England. They
spelt *herichon* a number of wrong ways before finally settling on *urchin,* and they called the hedgehog an urchin for
a time. They also applied the name urchin to a mischievous
child, because the urchin or hedgehog was popularly believed to be a mischievous elf in disguise. Eventually people stopped using urchin as a synonym for hedgehog, but
not for an impish child. Neither was the name *sea urchin*
abandoned, this spiny creature originally named for its resemblance to the urchin or hedgehog and once called the
sea hedgehog.

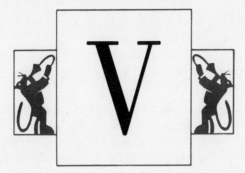

VETERINARIAN

That this word for an expert animal doctor derives from the Latin *veterinarius*, "belonging or pertaining to beasts of burden," which in turn comes from *veterina animalia*, "beasts of burden" (probably from *vetus*, "old"), shows that veterinarians originally cared exclusively for farm animals. Several rare names for veterinary used through history are *emplastrist* (for the plasters they used), *unguentarian* (for their ointments), *hippo-jatrist* (hippo = horse), and *hippologist* (though this strictly means anyone well versed in the study of horses). Other names that are rarely if ever used anymore are *horse doctor* and *horse leech*. Veterinarian was in the seventeenth century also the name for a man who rented out horses or mules, like Hobson of *Hobson's choice* (*q.v.*). *Vet*, a synonym for veterinarian today, has in recent years become a verb meaning to treat or cure as a veterinary does, as where an editor

217

vets a manuscript. An old joke tells about the doctor who was asked by an ill-tempered judge if he had ever been a veterinarian. "Why, yes," he replied. "Are you sick?"

VIRGIL'S FLY; VIRGIL'S GNAT

Legend has it that the Roman poet Virgil's (70–19 B.C.) "pet housefly" was given a funeral that cost over $100,-000. Musicians, mourners, and eulogists were hired and Virgil's mansion was declared the fly's mausoleum. Later it was discovered that Virgil buried the fly so that he could prevent the state from confiscating his estate and distributing it to war veterans as payment for service—all family cemetery plots and mausoleums being exempt from such confiscation. History confirms that Virgil's property was confiscated and that he got it back, but tells us nothing about his pet housefly. Many medieval legends arose about Virgil, and though this story may be true, it probably has its basis in Virgil's real troubles with his property, plus a tale that he allegedly wrote called the "Culex." Spenser wrote a poem called "Virgil's Gnat," based on the "Culex," in which a sleeping shepherd is stung by a gnat, which has bitten him only to warn him that he is about to be attacked by a serpent. The shepherd kills the gnat and then slays the dragon, but the next night the gnat reproaches him for his cruelty and the remorseful shepherd builds a monument honoring the gnat.

TO WARM THE COCKLES
OF ONE'S HEART

There are three good explanations for the *cockles* in this expression. The most popular, probably because it is the best story, says that late-seventeenth-century anatomists noticed the resemblance of the shape of cockleshells, the valves of a scalloplike mollusk, to the ventricles of the heart and referred to the latter as cockles. Others have sought the word's derivation in *corculum,* the Latin diminutive for heart, and in the Latin phrase *cochleae cordis,* ventricles of the heart. The first recorded use of the expression supports the last theory, but that slim evidence is all that has been found anywhere. Whatever the case, *cockles* isn't used anymore except in the expression *to warm the cockles of one's heart,* to please someone immensely, to evoke a glow of pleasure or a feeling of affection. Formerly, the cockles of the heart could be pleased, delighted, made to rejoice, or be comforted, as in "My cockles are comforted whenever I enter the door" (Southey). Behind each expression is the old scientific and poetical belief that the heart was the seat of the affections.

WELSH RABBIT

Welsh rarebit is entirely wrong as the name for melted seasoned cheese poured over buttered toast. But rather than being an affected, mannered corruption of the correct *Welsh rabbit,* it is a well-meaning, if misdirected, attempt to remove a slur on Welshmen from the language. *Welsh rabbit,* country humor dating back to Shakespeare's time, conveys the idea that only people as poor and stupid as the Welsh would eat cheese and call it *rabbit,* while the much later Welsh rarebit of restaurant menus makes the Welsh dish a rare and tasty bit. But *rarebit* is an artificial, invented word used in no other connection. At any rate, the Welsh are England's native Celts. Called *wealhs,* "foreigners," by the invading Saxons, of all people, they were driven off into the western hills and their green valleys. *Wealhs* became *Welsh* in time and these inhabitants of Wales suffered almost as much abuse at the hands and from the tongues of the English as did the Scottish or Irish. Their traditional enemies used *Welsh* to signify anything poor, stupid, or crooked, such as *a Welsh comb* (the fingers), *a Welsh carpet* (a painted floor), *to welsh,* and *Welsh rabbit.* Even the ancient word *walnut* is a kind of slur on the Welsh—it comes from the Anglo-Saxon *wealhhnutu,* "the foreign or Welsh nut." Other dishes humorously or contemptuously named for a people include *Scottish woodcock,* scrambled eggs on toast spread with anchovy butter, *Scotch coffee,* hot water flavored with burned toast, and *Cape Cod turkey,* codfish.

WHISTLING RHINOS AND
OTHER NOISY ANIMALS

The vulture and stork are silent animals without sound boxes and unable to speak, though the vulture is often said to scream in story and fable. But many, if not most, animals do make sounds that have been represented in various ways by human beings who have heard them. The following collection of names given to animal cries, a good beginning, is far from complete and, I suspect, inaccurate or dead wrong in some cases (I've never heard a giraffe bleat or a rhinoceros whistle!). Additions and corrections to and about these barbaric yawps and nasal groans are welcome:

    Albatrosses—nasal groan (*ah-h-h*) when mating
    Apes—gibber
    Asses—bray
    Bears—growl
    Bees—hum, buzz, murmur
    Beetles—drone
    Birds—sing
    Bitterns—boom
    Blackbirds—whistle
    Bulls—bellow
    Calves—bleat
    Cats—mew, purr, caterwaul, swear
    Chickens—peep, cackle
    Cocks—crow
    Cows—moo, low

Crows—caw
Cuckoos—cuckoo
Deer—bell
Dogs—bark, bay, howl, yelp, snarl, woof, arf
Dolphins—click
Doves—coo, moan
Ducks—quack
Eagles—scream
Elephants—trumpet
Falcons—chant
Flies—buzz
Foxes—bark, yelp
Frogs—croak
Geese—cackle, hiss, honk
Giraffes—guttural bleats and grunts
Grasshoppers—chirp, pitter
Grouse—drum
Guinea fowl—cry ("come back")
Guinea pigs—squeak, whistle
Gulls—squawk
Hares—squeak
Hawks—scream
Hippopotamuses—bray, snort
Horses—neigh, whinny
Hyenas—laugh
Jays—chatter
Kittens—mew
Linnets—chuckle
Lions—roar, growl
Loons—blood-chilling, maniacal howl
Magpies—chatter
Mice—squeak, squeal
Monkeys—chatter, gibber
Nightingales—pipe, warble, "jug-jug"
Owls—hoot, screech (actually wail softly)
Oxen—low, bellow

Parrots—talk
Peacocks—scream
Peewits—cry ("peewit")
Penguins—babies bleat, adults seldom utter a sound
Pigeons—coo
Pigs—grunt, squeal, squeak
Ravens—croak
Rhinoceroses—snort, grunt, growl, whistle
                    (female to male when in heat)
Rooks—caw
Sandpipers—pipe or whistle
Shearwaters—shrill eerie cry that led to tales of
                    haunted isles
Sheep—baa, bleat
Snakes—hiss
Sparrows—chirp
Stags—bellow, call
Swallows—titter
Swans—cry (sing before death, according to legend),
          hiss, grunt, bark
Thrushes—whistle
Tigers—roar, growl
Tortoises—grunt (in courtship only)
Turkeys—gobble
Wolves—howl

WHITE ELEPHANT

Long ago, the king of Siam, who held the title Lord of the
White Elephants, was considered the owner of all the rare
albino elephants in his kingdom, and since they were sacred to him, only he could ride, work, or destroy such an
animal. Infant white elephants were brought to the court
where human wet nurses suckled them. They were fed

such rich food that they often died of indigestion. The old story is that whenever the king wanted to punish one of his courtiers he simply gave one of his white elephants to him—the white elephant eating his luckless victim out of house and home. This story is the source of our expression a *white elephant*—any possession that is useless, eats up money, and can't be gotten rid of—even though no one has ever found any evidence of a king of Siam indulging in any such maleficent munificence. Perhaps the story is true nevertheless. It may have been concocted in the seventeenth century, at about the time that Siam's albino elephants became known in England. Indeed, at that time England's Charles I was presented with an elephant (not a white one, but an elephant accompanied by five camels to offset this slight) by the king of Siam. Charles was hard up for money then and didn't appreciate the cost of keeping his gift. This was estimated at £275 a year, a lot of the money going for the gallon of wine his keepers insisted the elephant had to drink in place of water every day. Such a diet must have resulted in a lot of *borborygmus,* the wonderful word for loud rumblings in the intestine. The elephant, thanks to an inefficient digestive system, produces 175 gallons or more of gas a day!

TO WIN HANDS DOWN

A jockey who wins a race hands down is so far ahead of the field that he doesn't have to lift the reins to urge his horse forward and crosses the finish line with his hands down, letting up on the reins. From racetrack slang toward the end of the last century the metaphor *to win hands down* passed into general use for any easy, effortless victory, a walkover.

WINCHESTER GEESE

Prostitution and geese raising were two major Winchester industries in the sixteenth century, and British prostitutes were called *Winchester geese* because they seemed almost as ubiquitous in the area as the birds. The first part of their name may honor the bishop of Winchester, however, as the brothels in Southwark were under his jurisdiction, and the Church received rent from many establishments based in houses it owned—these revenues, incidentally, helping found and maintain a number of esteemed Oxford colleges. A Winchester goose also came to mean anyone infected with venereal disease.

WITH TAIL BETWEEN LEGS

When this expression was first figuratively applied no one knows, but it must have been long ago, for from as early as 1400 writers have described frightened dogs with their tails between their legs. The attitude of scared, cowardly dogs was transferred to any thoroughly cowed and abased person who stands back *with tail between legs*. The word *coward* is ultimately from the Latin *cauda,* "tail"; it may be an allusion to an animal cowering with its tail between its legs or "turning tail" and running.

WOOLGATHERING

In the past, and perhaps even today, people wandered the countryside gathering bits of wool from hedges and bushes that sheep had brushed against. These actual "woolgath-erers," often children, went about their work aimlessly, often frolicking in the fields, never able to do their job systematically because the sheep were scattered all over. There wasn't much money to be gained in such an occupation, either. So as far back as the sixteenth century this literal wool-gathering suggested our expression *woolgathering,* meaning unprofitable or trivial employment, absentmindedness, inattention, purposeless thinking, or aimless reverie.

TO WORK (OR PAY) A DEAD HORSE

If there was originally a story about a poor wight who put a down payment on a horse to help him plow his land, only to have the horse die in harness the first day and leave him with almost the whole cost of its purchase to pay, that tale is unfortunately lost. But it does seem that such a story inspired our expression *to work* (or *pay*) *a dead horse,* meaning to labor for something that doesn't exist. The expression is more than three centuries old and still used—as when a car without collision insurance is destroyed in an accident and the owner has to continue making the installment payments on it.

WORK INTO A LATHER

When we tell someone "Don't work yourself into a lather" over something, we mean don't get hot and bothered, don't get angry or worried. *Lather* derives from the Anglo-Saxon word for washing soda or foam and has long been used to describe the flecks of foam on a heavily perspiring horse. From the notion of a horse worked into a hot and bothered state came our expression, probably in the mid-nineteenth century.

WREN

For some unknown reason the Angles and Saxons believed that this little bird was more lascivious than any other and gave it the name *wraene,* their word for lascivious, which became our *wren* in time. Almost certainly whoever coined the acronym WRENS for *W*omens *R*oyal *N*aval *S*ervice, during World War I, had no knowledge of this etymology. The little five-inch-long house wren (*Troglodytes aedon*), which braves British winters, and many others of the family, figure largely in European folklore. Among the cruelest of traditions was Wrenning Day (December 26), when whole villages swarmed across the English countryside stoning wrens to death to commemorate St. Stephen's martyrdom. This was done, for some reason, because the first Christian martyr, accused of blasphemy, was stoned to death.

XANTHUS

According to the *Iliad,* Achilles' immortal horse Xanthus, who takes his name from the Greek for reddish gold, wept when Achilles' gentle friend Patroclus, who had taken Achilles' place on the battlefield, was killed by Hector while leading the Myrmidons into battle. When Achilles reprimanded him for leaving Patroclus on the field of battle, Xanthus reproachfully told his master that he would soon die, through no fault of his horse but by the decree of inexorable destiny. It is not likely that Xanthus gave his name to the Xanthus river, the ancient name of the Scamander. The river was probably called Xanthus, or reddish gold, because legend held that it so colored the fleece of sheep washed in its waters.

XYLOPHAGE

A *xylophage*, which takes its name from the Greek *xylo*, "wood," and *phagein*, "to eat," is any wood-eating insect, such as a termite. The adjective *xylophagous* means "feeding on wood" and usually refers to the teredo worm and other crustaceans, mollusks, and fungi that perforate or destroy timber.

YELLOW-DOG CONTRACT

The yellow dog, generally considered a common cur or
mongrel, has long been a symbol of utter worthlessness in
America, and the term *yellow dog* has been used in expressions of contempt since at least 1833, when it is first
so recorded. Toward the end of the nineteenth century it
began to be heard in the term *yellow-dog contract,* a contract in which company employees do not or cannot join
the union. Yellow-dog contracts were outlawed by the
Wagner Act in 1935, but the practice and expression still
linger.

YOU CAN'T MAKE A SILK PURSE
OUT OF A SOW'S EAR

By painstakingly using both silk fibers and the skin or hair of a sow's ear, a man actually did make a silk purse out of a sow's ear a few years back. But the expression means you can't make something good out of something naturally inferior in quality. George Herbert was the first to record an approximation of the old saying in *The Temple: Sacred Poems and Private Ejaculations* (1633), but Jonathan Swift first recorded it fully in *Polite Conversation* (1738).

ZOO

Zoo ultimately derives from the Greek word *zoion* for animal. But the little word more immediately owes its life to the Zoological Garden in Regent's Park, London, established in 1828 by the Zoological Society of London and stocked with animals from the royal menagerie that had formerly been kept at the Tower of London. Though this was the first zoo to be called a zoo when people started abbreviating Zoological Garden, it was by no means the first large collection of wild animals, the earliest known zoo dating back to the reign of the Chinese Emperor Wang in the eleventh century B.C., featuring animals from all China's provinces and called a "garden of intelligence." Aristotle had his own little zoo, stocked by Alexander the Great's army as it made its conquests throughout the world. The Romans had collections of wild animals, exceeding any in the world since the emperor Augustus alone collected 420 tigers, 260 lions, and 600 other African animals, including elephants, a rhinoceros, and a hippopotamus. There are great zoos all over the world today. A number thrive in the United States despite the lack of government interest, and funding, in this important area. These include the Milwaukee Country Zoo, the San Diego Zoo, and New York City's Bronx Zoo.

A ZOO FULL OF ANIMALS
NAMED AFTER PLACES AND PEOPLE

Afghan hound. Bred in Afghanistan since at least 3000 B.C., this large, slender, heavy-coated dog, related to the greyhound, was used by the Egyptians for hunting.

Airedale terrier. First called a *Bingley terrier* after the Bingley district in Yorkshire, England, the dog's name was officially changed to *Airedale* in 1886, the Aire river running through Bingley. *Terrier,* from the Latin *terra* ("earth"), means a dog that "takes the earth," in reference to the terrier digging into burrows to catch badgers and other prey.

Angora cat. Angora cats probably originated in Ancyra or Angora, Turkey (now Ankara), where their long, silky hair may have been used like wool. Bred in Angora two thousand years ago for its hair, sometimes called mohair, the *Angora goat* is now raised throughout the world.

Angora rabbit. Long-haired rabbits named after the Angora goat and also raised for their hair.

Bantam. The dwarf fowl takes its name from Bantam, Java, where it was developed, and gives its name to any little feisty person.

Bedlington terrier. Originated in Bedlington in England's Northumberland County and was once called the *Northumberland terrier.*

Boston terrier. A cross of bull terrier and bulldog bred in Boston, Massachusetts.

Brittany spaniel. Originated in Brittany, northwestern France. (See *Spaniel.*)

Calico bird. See *Calico cat.*

Calico cat. Calicut cloth from Calicut (also Kozhikode), India, was changed in speech over the years to *calico cloth.* In the early nineteenth century colorful printed calicos were very popular in America, and they gave their name to *calico cats,* spotted *calico horses,* variegated *calico salmon,* the red-spotted *calico crab,* the spotted *calico goldfish,* and the spotted turnstone or *calico bird,* not to mention a number of vegetables.

Cape Cod turkey. A humorous name in Massachusetts for codfish.

Clydesdale horse. This strong workhorse was bred in the valley of Scotland's upper Clyde River.

Cochin. A large fowl named after Cochin, China.

Dalmatian. The spotted coach dog and fire dog of the past originated in Dalmatia on what is now Yugoslavia's Adriatic Sea coast.

Finnan haddie. At the village of Finnan near Aberdeen, Scotland, haddock fish smoked in green wood became known in dialect as *Finnan haddie* and is celebrated far and wide for its good taste.

Great Dane. The tall, strong dog takes its name from Denmark, where the breed originated.

Guinea hen. The ancestor of today's tasty *guinea hen* hailed from Guinea in western Africa, unlike the *guinea pig* (*q.v.*).

Irish terrier. A terrier bred in Ireland.

Irish water spaniel. The tallest breed of all spaniels was originated in Ireland for retrieving.

Karakul sheep. A wiry, black-furred, fat-tailed sheep originally bred near Lake Karakul (Black Lake) in Russia's mountainous Tadzhik region.

Labrador. A smaller version of the *Newfoundland* (*q.v.*), named after Labrador, Canada.

Lakeland terrier. A terrier named for England's Cumberland County lake region.

Leghorn chicken. The big egg producer hails from Livorno, Italy, which in English is *Leghorn.*

Lhasa apso terrier. The "forbidden city" of Lhasa in Tibet gave its name to this long-haired terrier bred as far back as the twelfth century.

Littleneck clam. Probably from Little Neck Bay, Long Island, New York.

Maltese spaniel. An ancient breed of spaniel originated on the island of Malta.

Manx cat. Hails from the Isle of Man.

Newfoundland. The big shaggy dog comes from the island of Newfoundland.

Pekingese. A Chinese dog named for the Chinese city.

Persian lamb. Originally the pelts of fur from these lambs came from Russia and Asian countries, but now they might just as likely come from Texas.

Pomeranian dog. The little toy balls of hair were produced from many breeds (including big spitz sled dogs) in a northern province of Germany called Pomerania that is now mainly in Poland.

Saluki. The gazelle hound, named after Saluq, Arabia.

Sardine. After Sardinia.

Scottish terrier. A small terrier bred in the Scottish highlands.

Siamese cat. Named after Siam, though it may not have originated there.

Skye terrier. Developed on Scotland's Isle of Skye centuries ago.

Sussex spaniel. A spaniel from Sussex in southern England.

Tarantula. The spider takes its name from the Italian seaport Taranto.

Turkey. So named because the American fowl reached England via Turkey.

Welsh spaniel. This spaniel was bred in Wales.

Yorkshire terrier. A toy breed from Yorkshire, England.

PEOPLE-NAMED ANIMALS

Several animals named after real people have full entries in these pages, but there are hundreds more, not including eponymous animals named after mythical persons such as the *rhesus monkey,* named for Rhesus, the mythological king of Thrace. The English, for example, once called the fox a *Charley* after the clever politician Charles James Fox; and the Carib Indians of South America, thought to be cannibals, give their name to a carnivorous fish of America, the *caribe* (also called piranha). In New Zealand a wild pig is known as a *Captain Cook* in honor of the English explorer, who introduced pigs there. A Philippine fish is called the *lapulapu* after the treacherous king of Cebu, who had the explorer Magellan ambushed and killed. Two more familiar eponyms are *Père David's deer* and *Przewalski's horse.*

The scientific name of a recently discovered fish has an amusing story behind it. While fishing in the Gulf of Lower California novelist John Steinbeck and his friend "Doc" Ricketts noticed a little fish that lives in the cloaca of the sea cucumber and keeps darting in and out of the creature's anus. They named the hitherto unrecorded fish after Walter Winchell. *Proctophilus winchelli* is probably the only fish named after a gossip columnist, and probably one too many as far as Winchell was concerned.

The person with the most animals named in his honor

may be American biologist Alexander Wetmore, whose name appears in the scientific names of some forty animals, these ranging from a tropical bat to an Antarctic fish. Another namesake champion is Dr. Carl L. Hubbs, a renowned American marine scientist, who has twenty-two species of fish, a bird, a crab, a whale, two mollusks, two insects, three species of algae, and a research institute named after him. His wife and assistant, Laura, has a minnow and a lantern fish named in her honor.

ZOO OF THE FUTURE: THE SQUISH, BANDERSNATCH, ET CETERA

These may not be imaginary animals. They are to be seen at the Smithsonian Institution's Air and Space Museum, where there is a permanent exhibit of twenty-seven paintings of animals that might be found someday in outer space—a kind of zoo of the future based on educated guesses. The *bandersnatch* is a 10,000-pound centipede, the *great filter bat* a 150-pound flying rodent, and the *squish* a cross between a squid and a shark. We'll probably need such exotics to replace the animal species on earth that will be becoming extinct at the rate of *one a minute* by 1990, according to some expert estimates.

ZYZZYVA

A leaf-hopping insect that is often destructive to plants, the *zyzzyva* (pronounced ziz-ih-vuh) weevil of tropical America is one of the best examples of onomatopoeia at work in the creation of words. The dictionaries give its origin as "obscure," if they give it at all, but the word probably ultimately derives from the Spanish *zis, zas!*, which is "echoic of the impact of a blow," the reference being, of course, to the noise made by these cicadalike insects.

May all the animals in this book live as long as the words and phrases they inspired.

Robert Hendrickson is a widely published writer whose poems and stories have appeared in many literary quarterlies. The winner of a MacDowell Colony Fellowship, he is the author of eleven books, including *Human Words,* which was selected as an American Ambassador book by the English Speaking Union. His most recent book, *The Literary Life and Other Curiosities,* was highly praised as an entertaining compendium about writers and writing.